DARK
HOUR
OF
NOON

DARK
HOUR
OF
NOON

by Christine Szambelan-Strevinsky

J. B. LIPPINCOTT   New York

Library of Congress Cataloging in Publication Data

Szambelan-Strevinsky, Christine.
Dark hour of noon.
SUMMARY: A young Polish girl becomes involved
with anti-German underground activities
during World War II.
    1. World War, 1939–1945—Juvenile fiction.
[1. World War, 1939–1945—Underground movements—
Poland—Fiction. 2. Poland—Fiction] I. Title.
PZ7.S9867Dar   [Fic]   81-48601
ISBN 0-397-32013-2   ISBN 0-397-32014-0 (lib. bdg.)

1 2 3 4 5 6 7 8 9 10
First Edition

For Jeannette Cassin, teacher

Prologue

On September 1, 1939, the German army crossed the Polish borders. Forty-four days later the German takeover was complete. World War II had begun.

During their brutal five-year reign in Poland, the SS liquidated the Jews in Lodz, Kraków, Radom, and other cities. The largest, and most infamous massacre took place in the Warsaw ghetto. Here the Christian population was tyrannized as well.

On August 1, 1944, a year after the total destruction of the Warsaw ghetto, the Polish people launched a disastrous action known as the Polish Rising. During the course of the insurrection, the Polish Home Army (encouraged by the government-in-exile in London) attempted to seize Warsaw. Of the two hundred thousand Poles who participated in the action, ten thousand were killed and seven thousand were wounded before the rebellion was crushed by the Germans. The uprising terminated on October 2, 1944.

Total Polish casualties during this rising were over two hundred thousand, and nine-tenths of Warsaw was destroyed.

In Poland, the resistance movement was not limited to well-organized "official" groups. During the course of the war there were many individual acts of heroism that went unnoticed. The least known of these acts were those performed by the children of Poland.

1

September 1, 1939, was a sparkling prelude to autumn, as orange and gold as only a late summer day in Poland can be. There was a sharp tang of smoke in the air, piles of jewel-toned leaves crackled in the gutters, and delicate threads of *babie lato,* spun by minute spiders, drifted in the breeze.

Apartment three at number fourteen Polanska Street, the home of the Szumkowski family, was a whirlwind of activity. Aunts, uncles, and assorted cousins had gathered there to celebrate Ronka's nameday. Even old *baba* Toria, who seldom left home anymore, had come. There would be a gigantic party that night.

As usual, Ronka was in charge. She moved busily about the kitchen, mixing batter, frying *pączki,* basting the big ham purchased from Poznań's finest butcher's, and giving orders left and right. Kasia, the Szumkowskis' servant girl, hurried about the dining room, setting out china. This was the first time she had been trusted to place the crystal glasses. They stood sparkling, one at each setting, ruby, emerald, and sapphire. The newly polished candlesticks were fitted with fresh candles. The carpeting was spotless. The furniture gleamed from a combination of polish and elbow grease. Kasia paused to admire her handiwork. Yes, this was going to be a beautiful party.

Out on the balcony, Trina, a solemn-faced child of seven with long brown braids, sat dangling her legs through the railings, impatiently scanning the street. She was watching for Tosh to round the corner. Tosh was Trina's father, but she had never called him *Tata,* or Papa, or anything but Tosh.

As Trina sat waiting she hummed to herself, her hands idly assembling a boutonniere out of the asters she had picked from the long green boxes lining the balcony railings.

Somewhere in the background, barely audible above the hubbub emanating from the kitchen, the radio was playing. The rich voice of Jan Kiepura, the current operatic heartthrob, filled the apartment; he was singing an aria from *Halka.* His performance was interrupted by an announcer, who extolled the virtues of a household product. Then the tempo changed, and the Warsaw Choir launched into a medley of folk songs.

Suddenly the music stopped. After a brief silence, Trina heard strange whistlings and hootings emerging from the room where the mahogany radio cabinet stood. A voice barked out, speaking so rapidly that the words tumbled over one another: ". . . Crossed the border at . . . *hoot* . . . *screech* . . . tanks rolling across the bridge at . . . river . . . *wheee* . . . *crackle* . . ."

Silence again; then somebody screamed. Trina winced as the cry bored into her ears like the sound of a dentist's drill.

"Did you hear that? Germany's declared war!"

There was a burst of excited voices. Then the announcer continued, "Today, in an unprecedented act of aggression, the German army crossed the Polish borders . . . *screeeech* . . . planes have been spotted flying in the direction . . . *crackle* . . . *crackle* . . . Warsaw is being aerially attacked at this very moment . . ."

Trina looked up at the sky. As if by magic, planes appeared overhead. As she watched, puffs of smoke blossomed in the brilliant blue above. Trina heard whistles, sirens, and the sound of running feet. Then Ronka hurried out onto the balcony and took her by the arm.

"What's the matter? *Mamusia,* what's happening? When is Tosh coming home? *Mamusia,* what's wrong?" Trina babbled.

Ronka was far too distracted to answer her daughter. She hurriedly pushed Trina into a chair, and

5

then with her usual authority began issuing orders. "Helenka, take the children down to the *piwnica.* They'll be safe there in the basement. Take some pillows and blankets, you may be in the cellar for quite a while. And Trina, don't forget your sweater, it's cold down there. Go with your Aunt Helenka. Hurry."

Trina watched as her mother raked manicured fingers through her carefully waved hair. Ronka then turned her attention to the sniffling servant girl.

"Kasia, get some candles ready. Make some sandwiches. Use the ham. And quit that blubbering, girl. The Germans aren't here yet. Now, get going!"

Kasia gave a wail and threw her apron over her face, but managed a strangled "Yes, ma'am" before fleeing to the kitchen in search of candles and sandwich makings.

Tosh's older sister, Helenka, with her two small children, Grazia and Rys, in tow, began to gather up bedding. When her arms were full, she signaled Trina to follow her down the stairs to the basement. As they hurried along they could hear anxious murmurs and snatches of radio bulletins emerging through their neighbors' open doors: ". . . Skirmish at . . . woods . . . casualties at present unknown . . . heavy transport lorries moving in the vicinity . . . damage sustained in . . . cavalry regiment has been mowed down by an advancing Panzer division . . ." The somber voices pursued them all the way down to their *piwnica,* one of a series of interconnected basements.

In the Szumkowskis' kitchen, confusion reigned. Stella, one of Tosh's younger sisters, was pouring coffee into thermos bottles and trying to soothe *baba* Toria. The old woman was sick with worry because her son had not returned. "Don't worry, *mamusia,*" Stella kept saying. "Tosh will be here soon. You'll see. Now, why don't you go downstairs and help Helenka with the children? We'll follow you in a few minutes. Go, *mamusia.* And take the coffee with you."

Within fifteen minutes everybody except Ronka was in the basement. Helenka had settled the children on chairs that Uncle Staszek had carried downstairs. Stella was pouring out coffee and cocoa. Kasia was lighting candles, heeding her mistress's instructions not to burn too many at once. *Baba* Toria had taken over a corner chair and sat with little Rys in her lap; rosary beads slipped through her fingers and her lips moved silently.

Everyone looked up as Ronka and Professor Wronski, a neighbor from the first floor, came through the door. They were trundling the mahogany radio cabinet between them. Ronka's neck was festooned with coils of wire. After the radio had been

7

set up in the middle of the room, Ronka began stringing the cord along the floor. As she worked her way
back through the doorway she called over her shoulder, "I'll plug this in at the concierge's lodge. Then
we'll be able to keep up with what's going on."

". . . Coming . . . coming . . . now over the . . .
passed . . . coming . . ." The announcer's voice
droned on and on, pinpointing the bombing attacks.
Each new wave of aircraft was preceded by "Coming
. . . coming . . . coming . . ." The planes' depar-
tures were followed by "Passed . . . passed . . ."

Trina huddled in her chair, hugging a pillow. Candlelight flickered on the damp brick walls, sending
shadows dancing across the vaulted ceiling. The
sound of voices rose and fell. The cellar was more
crowded now that the professor's wife, Maryla,
and his daughter, Janka, had joined him underground.

Trina shivered. Where was Tosh? Why didn't he
come? Didn't he know she needed him? That she
was afraid? She gathered her pillow closer, feeling
misery envelop her like an invisible cloak.

Then suddenly Tosh was there, and everything
was all right again. He scooped her up in his arms
and settled down in a chair. Secure on her father's
lap, Trina slept. With Tosh close by it no longer
mattered so much that sirens were wailing and explosions were shaking the walls.

———

When Trina woke up, it was night. She rubbed her eyes and looked about her. Grazia and Rys lay stretched out on a row of chairs. Uncle Staszek sat with his ear to the radio, smoking a pipe. Janka was trying to read by the flickering candlelight. Kasia was rocking to and fro, sniffling and muttering to herself. The professor and his wife were playing cards. *Baba* Toria snored gently with her mouth hanging open. Aunt Helenka and Aunt Stella were talking together in soft voices. . . .

Somebody was missing. *Mamusia!* Trina stirred and felt Tosh's arms tighten around her. "Shh! *Maleńka.* Little one. *Mamusia* will be back in a minute," he whispered, exactly as if he could read Trina's mind. "She'll be right back, and she'll bring you a piece of her nameday cake and some Ovaltine. Just wait, you'll see."

While Trina dozed in her father's arms, Ronka made countless trips up to the third floor and back, carrying down platefuls of the apple coffee cake for which she was justly famous, poppy seed rolls, stacks of ham sandwiches, bowls of potato salad. This was her nameday, and by God she would have her party, war or no war, bombs or no bombs. "Ronka, please stay here where it's safe," Tosh implored each time she headed upstairs. But Ronka insisted that she wasn't afraid.

After one of her trips to the apartment she handed

Tosh a map of Poland and a red crayon. "This will help us keep track of where the bastards are," she said, wiping perspiration from her forehead. "It's just like fireworks up there. The railroad station's burning—you can see it from our bedroom window."

All that night Ronka moved back and forth, bringing news: "Another fire . . . explosions to the north . . . the army base . . ." The radio droned on. It was well after dawn when the announcer finally sounded the all clear. The first day of the war had ended.

Morning found the streets of Poznań eerily still. Pedestrians hugged the walls, walking as quickly as possible to their destinations. Knots of people knelt on the pavements receiving absolution and communion from black-robed priests. An air of silent hysteria gripped the city.

Trina's household reflected the general quiet. By noon Aunt Helenka, her husband, and the children had left for their apartment across town, taking *baba* Toria and Stella with them. Stella would have to stay with them until rail service to her hometown was resumed. Kasia was also gone. After asking to be dismissed she had taken off for her own village, by heaven knew what means, since no public transportation was functioning.

By the end of the day Ronka had finished putting away the party things. She had taken time out now and then to study the map of Poland that Tosh had tacked to the living room wall. With each news bulletin the red crayon line had crept eastward, gulping up towns one by one. . . .

That evening Tosh's third sister, Winka, arrived from the nearby town of Gniezno with her three little boys in tow. "We're evacuating," she announced. "We're going to the country near Stella's village where there's no danger. Come with us," she urged Tosh and Ronka. "It isn't safe here. You'll see, the Germans will—"

"The *Szwabs* will, the *Szwabs* won't," Ronka snapped. "At least we're with our own people here. Who knows what might happen someplace else?"

Seeing the indecision in Tosh's face, she added, "If you want to go, go. But I'm not budging. Period. End of discussion. I'd rather meet the devil on my own home ground."

The Szumkowskis could not persuade Winka to stay in Poznań, and early the next morning she and the three little boys departed with much weeping and hugging. Tosh took them to the train. Rail service had been resumed, though the trains ran only sporadically.

During the next few days Ronka rounded up all the family's valuables she could carry and stashed them in places known only to herself. She also stocked the larder and bought several pairs of warm underwear for each of them. Her hair, usually coiffed

11

to perfection, frizzed out about her head. Trina thought that her mother resembled the chicken in the zoo—the one with the curly feathers.

Time and events were to confirm Ronka's premonitions. While life in Poznań and other cities soon returned to something like normal, the surrounding countryside became a battlefield. Misfortunate evacuees found themselves caught between the retreating Polish army and the advancing Germans. When Winka arrived at the Szumkowski's door two weeks later, with bloody rags encircling her head, followed by her bruised and bandaged boys, she had nothing but horror stories to relate. Only a few kilometers out of Poznań her train full of women and children had been strafed by German planes flying so low that she'd been able to make out the pilots' grinning faces.

"How could they have deliberately machine-gunned us that way?" she asked again and again. "Our trains were clearly marked with red crosses."

"I should have listened to you," she insisted, clutching at Ronka's arm. "You were absolutely right. When we ran from the train to the ditch I got separated from the boys—I couldn't find them for hours. I thought I'd lost my babies for good. They even shot at us in the ditch—in the *ditch,* while we lay there in the mud! I don't understand it— they could see we weren't soldiers! Why did they do it? Why?"

Stella showed up a week later. Her story matched Winka's. While she'd been on her way home, her train, too, had been attacked.

"I'm lucky to be here at all," she confided. "So many were hit . . . so many were killed. When we took cover in a haystack they dropped something on us to make the hay burn. That's how I lost my hair."

Even *baba* Toria, who had thought the family should flee the city, was forced to admit that her daughter-in-law had been right to stay. Though the admission was grudgingly made, Ronka felt a certain grim satisfaction. Praise from old *baba* Toria was praise indeed!

2

During the next few weeks, the city settled into a new routine. German patrols were everywhere, their presence proclaimed by the ringing sound of boots against the pavements. Ration cards appeared. All adults were ordered to register with the police, state the number of rooms in their houses, turn in their radios, and declare their professions. An uneasy quiet reigned.

Ronka and Tosh argued about the radio. "Hide it in the attic. Tosh, we must know what's going on!"

"Do you want me to go to jail? Be reasonable, Ronka. People are always going up there to rummage around in their trunks. We simply can't risk it."

Before long an underground newspaper was circulating from hand to hand. "It's lucky *somebody* kept their radio," Ronka said pointedly. "How else could they pass on the news?"

The Szumkowskis learned with delight that France had joined the war, then all too soon with dismay that France had fallen. Britain's entry into the war brought a new surge of optimism, but again hope waned when it became evident that a Britain under siege by the Germans could do nothing to rescue the rest of Europe. Gloom settled in.

Snow fell early and lay untouched and immaculate for days on end. The usual sledders stayed away from the customary hills; there wasn't a snowman or a snowball fight to be seen. Trina, bundled up by Ronka in layers of woolen clothing, booted and mittened, was sent outdoors to "get some roses into your cheeks." She hugged the entranceway, begging to be let in before the *Szwabs* got her. The moment Ronka opened the door, she was back in the house.

Nobody looked forward to Christmas that year. The invaders had stripped the shops bare of their holiday gifts and goodies, and food was in short supply. Moreover, people were disappearing daily from their homes. The Germans had solved the problem of housing the occupation forces in a very simple way. Each night, unfortunate families were awakened by a sudden knock at the door. A group of Gestapo men would be standing on the threshold in full regalia, guns at the ready. The terrified occupants would be told that they had fifteen minutes—sometimes less—to pack what they could. Then they would be hustled outside and into an open truck. The truck, they were told, would take them to an internment camp. What happened after that nobody knew.

Ronka grimly prepared for a midnight rap at the door. She packed all she could into the least possible space, choosing each item carefully. Practicality won out over sentimentality, and treasured possessions were laid aside in favor of warm clothing, enameled tinware, soap, and antiseptics. She abandoned her usual stylish dresses for men's trousers and heavy boots.

"When they come to get us I'm not going to be caught in silk stockings and high heels," she declared. "You make sure you wear your long johns under your pants, Tosh. And you, Trina, keep that sweater on. And don't forget your woolly stockings."

Ronka's kitchen window looked out on the back of the building that had become Gestapo headquarters. After watching the comings and goings day after day, Ronka became quite adept at predicting what each night would hold.

As the days dragged on, the Szumkowskis acquired the habit of dropping in to the professor's place at night. While Janka amused Trina in one corner, the grown-ups gathered about the massive dining table.

First Ronka would give her eyewitness report of Gestapo goings-on; then Tosh would read aloud from the "Toilet Paper." (The underground newspaper had quickly earned that nickname because of the limp, flimsy paper on which it was printed.) An animated discussion would follow. What did the future hold? Who would win the war? After one particularly heated exchange about Hitler, Tosh raced upstairs and, in a totally uncharacteristic fit of anger, shaved off his pencil-thin mustache.

One night in early January the Szumkowskis were, as usual, at the professor's. Ronka was pacing the floor. "I think it's our turn tonight," she said to no one in particular.

"Impossible," Tosh protested. "It's much too late. They usually stop after one, and it's nearly two A.M. now."

"I still think our time has come," Ronka said. "I can feel it in my bones. Mark my words. They'll be here!"

"Ronka, Ronka," Tosh chided. "Don't be so pessimistic. They have to rest sometime. I'm sure we're safe for tonight."

Ronka shook her head. "I'm going upstairs to get ready!"

Almost before the words were out of her mouth there was a pounding at the door.

"Gestapo! Open up!"

Ronka scooped up the "Toilet Paper" and ran to the bathroom to flush away the evidence. A moment later the professor's wife opened the door to admit the Germans. As the men filed in, Janka sat down at the piano and began pounding out the Polish national anthem. "Poland is not lost yet," she sang defiantly, "as long as we live. . . ."

Eight soldiers glared at Janka, machine guns poised. Then their officer began barking out orders. "Pack your things, *Herr* Professor," he snapped. "That goes for your wife and daughter, too."

The armed men fanned out into the apartment and found Ronka seated on the toilet.

"You! What are you doing there?"

"What does it look like I'm doing?" she retorted. "Would you care to inspect the bowl for contraband?"

Within minutes, the professor and his family were marched outside and put into a waiting truck, which quickly rumbled away. Tosh and Ronka, trailed by Trina, went upstairs in shocked silence. They gathered in the kitchen while Ronka made hot chocolate.

"They'll be back," Ronka said tonelessly. "Toshek, put the suitcases beside the door. Get our coats ready. Scarves, hats, mittens . . ."

Ronka's voice trailed off. She stood for a moment looking about her. Suddenly she stamped her foot on the floor. "I'm damned if I'll leave those devils anything I don't have to. My jams, my pickled mushrooms, all my other—" She paused, wrinkling her forehead in thought. In the next instant her face brightened.

"Trina, come with *mamusia,*" she cried, heading for the pantry. "Hurry, little one! Gather up these jars and follow me."

Her arms full of glass containers, Ronka headed for the kitchen. After dumping the jars on the table, she marched to the window and flung it wide open. Cold air rushed in. "Come here, Trina," she said urgently. "We're going to play a game. See how far and how hard you can throw these." And with that Ronka heaved a containerful of preserves out into the night.

"That takes care of the pickled peaches, my pet. And what have we here? Raspberry jam? Good!"

Another trip into the pantry. Crash after crash resounded from the courtyard below. "Come on, girl," Ronka hissed. "Throw something, quick!" Trina stared into her mother's glittering eyes, a bit afraid of this strange *mamusia.*

For a solid hour Ronka, with Trina's help, tossed jars full of fruit and vegetables through the open window. When there were no more preserves to throw, Ronka turned to Tosh's collection of fine wines. Tosh watched in silence. The one time he protested, Ronka hushed him impatiently.

Finally the pantry shelves were empty, but still Ronka did not stop. "I almost forgot. . . . They'll get nothing, nothing at all. Follow me, Trina." And she trotted off to the dining room. She opened the buffet and began to remove the crystal glasses, the elegant china plates, the goblets trimmed with gold. "We'll smash everything, by God!" Ronka's cheeks were flaming from exertion. Trina, caught up in her mother's excitement, nodded vigorously. She thought how pretty the colored glass must look on the white snow in the courtyard, and wished it was light so she could see it there.

Finally, her fury spent, Ronka sat down at the kitchen table. It was still dark outside.

"Don't you think we should go to bed?" Tosh asked. "It's nearly morning."

Ronka shivered. "I don't think we'll ever sleep in our beds again. I don't think— Listen!"

Familiar sounds drifted in through the windows: marching boots, running motors, guttural commands barked in German. "This is it," Ronka said grimly. "Do you think we'll ever see this place again?" Before Tosh could answer, she whispered, "I wonder." Then, squaring her shoulders, she patted Trina's head. "Chin up, little one," she said. "Look those *Szwab* bastards straight in the eye."

There was a loud knocking sound—the unmistakable pounding of gun butts on wood. Ronka strode to the door and flung it open. The same squad of Germans that had visited the building earlier filled the doorway. The one with the officer's insignia began to read from an official-looking document in his hand.

"Why don't you spare us that garbage?" Ronka demanded. "We know damned well why you're here, *gentlemen.*" Her voice dripped sarcasm.

One of the soldiers made a threatening gesture with his Mauser, but the officer waved him back. "*Nein, nein.* No need for that," he said.

At the sight of the troopers and guns, Trina started to tremble. Her eyes filled with tears, and she began edging behind her mother. Ronka grasped her arm. "Don't you ever let me see you cry in front of these *Szwabs!*" she hissed fiercely. "You're a Pole. Remember that! Don't you ever, ever cry!" Her fingers dug into Trina's flesh.

Trina glanced up at her mother. Ronka's mouth was set in a thin straight line. Her blue eyes were blazing. "*Mamusia* is very angry," Trina thought. "Angry—but not frightened." Trina set her own lips and stared hard at the Germans.

"*Das Kind,* the child, she is afraid?" the officer asked.

"Afraid? Why should she be afraid of a cockroach like you?" Ronka snapped, gathering coats as she spoke. "May your children spit on your grave," she added. "May your mother curse forever the day she bore you! May your bones lie unburied and rotting far from home!"

The officer stood listening, his face impassive. Tosh frantically signaled Ronka to be still, but she ignored him. As they were being herded out the door and down the stairs, Ronka kept up a steady stream of insults.

Outside, in the last cold hours of the night, a truck stood waiting. It was filled almost to capacity. Ronka and Tosh handed Trina up then pulled themselves aboard. The truck took off into the darkness.

Someone began singing, slightly off key but with gusto, "Poland is not lost yet . . ." Other voices joined in. They finished the anthem and went into a parody of a Christmas carol that mocked the invaders. They were still singing when the truck rolled to a stop in front of the internment camp.

3

The sky was beginning to lighten as the truck drew up to the gates of the camp. After an exchange between the camp guards and the truck's Gestapo escorts, the gates were thrown open. The truck drove in. The tailgate was lowered, and soldiers motioned the passengers to get out. Slowly, numb with cold, they clambered down, dragging their few possessions behind them.

The barracks where they would live had once served as an arsenal. The long, twin-tiered wooden buildings were not insulated against the cold; snow drifted between chinks in the wall boards, and the wind whistled through. Icicles hung from the rafters. There were two concrete cold-water sinks in each of the buildings. Two small cast-iron stoves, well past their prime, provided the only heat. Each building housed five hundred people. The more fortunate ones slept in bunks on the upper tier, where it was a bit warmer. The others slept at ground level with only thin straw pallets between them and the bare concrete. The toilet facilities were outside—"multiple-holers" usually occupied to capacity.

Looking back on that time, Trina could not separate the days spent in the barracks into distinct units. The long weeks blended into one unrelieved blur of misery, cold, and hunger. Trina's only escape was in dreams. If she closed her eyes very tightly she could almost see the house back on Polanska Street: the grandfather clock in the parlor, chiming the hours (except when she hid inside, the weights at rest atop her head); the massive table with the lion's claw feet; the carved cabinet, its glass front gleaming, jars of ruby-red fruit and candy, tins of cookies, and pots of marmalade hidden behind its little carved doors; the samovar on its silver stand, steam whistling through the narrow spout. . . .

Trina's family was lucky compared to some—they drew one of the "penthouses" on the upper tier. The upper level was reached by a rickety stepladder, and was divided into stalls lining the walls. An open middle area looked down on the stoves and sinks grouped in the center of the floor below. The stalls looked like those found in stables. Each unit was occupied by about a dozen people. Strangers slept huddled together as much to pool their body warmth as because there was no space to spread out. Personal possessions were stowed against the walls for use as pillows and seats. In front of each stall stood a rough wooden table flanked by benches.

Food was issued twice a day. Breakfast consisted of a bowl of thin gruel and a cup of ersatz coffee. A bowl of watery soup containing unidentifiable floating objects, a chunk of black bread, and more ersatz coffee followed in the late afternoon. Some of the longtime barracks occupants had managed to contact relatives and were getting food packages. These packets formed the basis for a lively black market: so many cigarettes for the use of a metal cup to boil water in; an apple in exchange for a pair of woolen socks . . . Some enterprising souls grew rich in the process, obtaining gold wedding rings in return for smoked sausage, watches for jam. Little did they know that when they departed from the camp, their jailers would strip them of their newly acquired riches.

Ronka proved amazingly adept at black-market trading. "What am I bid for a nice sharp razor blade?" she'd cry. "What am I bid? Dried peaches? Who's going to bid higher? A link of sausage? Sold to the lady with the sausage! Now, here's a beauty:

a cake of real soap! Lilac perfumed! Almost as good as new, barely used. . . . Bacon? Fine, my friend, you have yourself a deal."

Whenever Ronka returned from her marketing ventures, Tosh would shake his head—half in amazement, half in disbelief. "Where did you learn to be such a bargainer?" he'd ask. "Just look at this stuff!"

"She has to eat," Ronka would reply, nodding toward Trina. "This pig slop they're feeding us runs right through her. And look at me! I'm at least sixty kilos thinner."

"You're still *zoftig,* Roneczka," Tosh would reply. "By the way, do you think you could get me some powdered charcoal? I've got the runs, too."

"There's a doctor in barracks four-A. Somebody said that he'd managed to bring in a whole suitcaseful of medicine. Let's see. This is a pretty good sweater. . . . Hmm, maybe. . . ." And Ronka would go off to barracks four-A in pursuit of the needed remedy.

Diarrhea was not the only health problem facing the internees. They also suffered from pneumonia and other assorted ills. But diarrhea was the most debilitating of their maladies. Five, ten, fifteen times a day Trina would depart on the run for the outhouses, only to find them fully occupied. There was nothing left to do but squat in the snow. On one such occasion Trina found herself crouched next to Professor Wronski's daughter, Janka. Forgetting the urgency of her cramping stomach, she threw her arms around her friend, toppling her to the ground. They had only a few minutes to speak before Trina had to race back to her own barracks.

"*Mamusia, mamusia!* Toshek! The professor and his family are down in twelve-H! Stall fourteen, bottom!" she shouted, jumping up and down. "Let's go see them now, please! Let's go now!"

"We will! We'll go right away."

Trina waited impatiently while Ronka and Tosh bundled themselves into layers of sweaters and coats for the long, cold walk. She was going to see her friends! From the old place, from home!

The former neighbors had a tearful reunion accompanied by kissing and hugging. The professor's wife, alerted by Janka, had prepared a veritable feast. There was hot oatmeal with real sugar! Stewed prunes and real tea! And when Trina mentioned that just a few days earlier she had turned eight, the professor stood up.

"This we must celebrate," he said. "I have something very special for you." And with that he held out a square of chocolate.

Trina was speechless. But her eyes spoke where words failed her, and the hug she gave the professor repaid him amply for his generosity.

Janka, not to be outdone by her father, also produced a present for Trina. While the little girl watched, fascinated, Janka fashioned a doll out of a piece of cloth, stuffed it with straw, and inked its features with a pen. Trina accepted the doll with delight. "I'm going to name her Marysia," she announced. "And I'm going to make her some warm clothes so she won't freeze in this cold." Settling down in a corner, she rocked and hugged her new doll, while the grown-ups' conversation flowed around her.

There was so much to talk about—from the unusual severity of this winter's weather to the best way of killing the lice (which were rampant in the camp). There was gossip about other inmates to exchange; there were jokes about Hitler and the war to tell. Time flew by, and soon the Szumkowskis had to leave their old friends and return to their own barracks. But the two families did not part until they had promised to exchange visits as often as possible.

The days dragged by, all of them alike except for the special times when the Szumkowskis and the Wronskis got together for a visit. And then there was an occasional inspection by the camp commandant. Word spread rapidly each time such an inspection was scheduled. With forewarning, the male inmates, who were required to doff their hats to the commandant, could arrange to be bareheaded before the officer appeared in their midst. Powerless as they were, it was one gesture of defiance they could make in the face of the enemy, and they took comfort from even so small a triumph.

As the long winter wore on, some of the barracks

were emptied only to be reoccupied by another group of grim-faced refugees. One day the professor and his family were gone, and something akin to despair settled over Trina's family. Then at last it was their turn to go. One bitterly cold March morning the commandant's deputies arrived in the Szumkowskis' barracks and proceeded to rout everybody out.

"*Raus! Raus! Sich ruhren!* Hurry! Hurry! Get going!" The guttural German shouts filled the air. "Move! Out! Out!"

Everyone hurriedly packed their few belongings. A column formed in the middle of the building. When the doors opened, the column headed out, moving like a disjointed snake. The group marched through the camp in the pallid morning light, feeling the unseen gaze of those being left behind. They crossed through the camp and up to a railroad siding. A train stood waiting—a motley string of Pullmans, cattle cars, and third-class coaches. Soldiers, their bayoneted Mausers at the ready, moved the column up to the car immediately behind the engine. The inmates were ordered inside. When the carriage was filled to the bursting point, its doors were locked and sealed, and the column moved on to the next car. One by one all the carriages were filled.

The Szumkowskis were lucky again. They drew one of the Pullmans and were as comfortable as anyone could expect under the circumstances.

"I wonder where we're going?" Tosh said.

"To hell! Where do you think?" a voice shouted. "Were you expecting a summer vacation?" Hoots of laughter greeted this retort. In spite of the uncertainty of their destiny, the group was seized with a type of gallows humor, and joke followed joke. Perhaps it was because *something* was finally happening—almost anything was preferable to the limbo they'd been in. But the gaiety in the crowded car was short-lived, for the train sat there . . . and sat . . . and sat. . . . It was three days before the engines started up. And for three more interminable days the exhausted passengers sat frozen in their seats as the train alternately rumbled and chugged along, traveling along sidings and spurs that seemed to lead to nowhere.

Finally the train stopped. When the doors opened Trina blinked in the unexpectedly brilliant light. They had drawn up in the center of a small town. Farmers in horse-drawn wagons were gathered in a circle around the long line of train cars. Breath steaming, collars raised, they watched from their wagon seats as the former inmates of the Poznań camp straggled off the train. Again the deportees were assembled into a column. Names were called out. As each family group stepped forward, a farmer drew up with his wagon and signaled the newcomers aboard. Then, one by one, the wagons pulled out.

———

30

4

Trina looked up at the wagon beside her. The young man sitting on the seat wore a fur jacket turned skin-side out and a cap with flaps over the ears. He was smoking a hand-rolled cigarette. After studying the Szumkowskis in silence, he spat, and with a flick of his whip indicated that they should get into the wagon. Tosh threw in their bundles, boosted Trina up, gave Ronka a helping hand, and climbed aboard himself. The driver slapped the reins against the horse's flanks and whistled through his teeth. The animal broke into a trot.

The young man glanced over his shoulder at his passengers, spat again, and asked, "What's your name?"

"Tosh Szumkowski. My wife, Ronka. My daughter, Trina."

"I'm Stefan," said the driver.

"Where are we heading?"

"Warznica. My house," the young man said tersely.

"Why are we going there?"

"*Niemcy.*"

"*Niemcy?* The Germans? I don't understand."

"They say we have to take you in."

"Oh!" Tosh thought for a while, digesting the information. "You mean they ordered you to house someone?"

"That's right."

"Did they give you a choice? Or did they just tell you who to take?"

"They call my name. Call your name."

Tosh flushed. "I see."

During this exchange, the horse plodded steadily along. The road was narrow and covered with rutted snow. Tosh looked about, trying to get his bearings. The surrounding trees were a mixture of pines, birches, and others. He could see other wagons proceeding across the hilly terrain. Stefan's cart rumbled by a crossroads shrine—a wooden cross surrounded by a sunburst of alpine flowers. Tosh could tell by the rugged little blooms that they were somewhere in the foothills of the Carpathian Mountains.

Finally the road widened slightly, and houses appeared. Warznica was a typical farming village—a main road bordered on both sides by houses. Each farmhouse was ringed by a picket fence. To the back of each lay a carefully tended courtyard with chicken coops, a barn, a manure pit, and outhouses. Small orchards and gardens lay beyond. These gave onto fields that stretched in all directions.

Halfway through the village the road belled out, then narrowed again. Facing this widening in the road stood the manor house, the *dwór,* a remnant of Poland's feudal past. (Tosh would later learn that its present owner, a descendant of the vanishing nobility, was the village's largest landowner and its only literate inhabitant.) There was no store, no church, no schoolhouse—those were all back in the town from which they had come.

The wagon came to a stop in front of a farmhouse. It was evident from the bright whitewash, the neatly painted fence, and what looked like it would be a flower garden in the summertime that the owner was a cut above the average peasant. Stefan pointed with his whip. "My house," he said. He snapped the reins and the horse turned into the open gates. The wagon drew up in the courtyard. Two young women, both with long blonde braids hanging past their waists, came out of the back door.

"*Siostry*—sisters." Then, indicating an obviously pregnant young woman who had appeared in the doorway: "My wife."

33

The girl on the threshold smiled uncertainly and made a vague gesture with her hands. "Come in, come in," she said. "It's so cold."

The Szumkowskis entered the house. They found themselves in a kitchen whose whitewashed walls matched the snow outside in brilliance. Along the edge of the low ceiling and around the window frames ran bright friezes of *wycinanki,* paper cutouts in the shapes of fantastic flowers and beasts. Fully one-fourth of the room was occupied by the oven, an enormous earthen structure typical of peasant houses. It was capable of holding at least a dozen loaves of bread as big as small wagon wheels. A ledge running alongside it served as a seat, a place to set pails of milk to clabber, and a shelf on which bread dough could rise. The oven top, reached by steps hewn into the clay, was the warmest spot in the house. It was here that old *babusia* slept on winter nights.

One side of the kitchen was taken up by a huge wooden table, scrubbed to pristine whiteness and flanked by benches. A marvelously carved chair was placed at its foot, another at its head. In one corner stood a china cabinet filled with a profusion of knick-knacks. Another corner contained a tub, for washing up; a pail of water with a wooden dipper; and a bucket for slops. On the windowsills stood small religious figurines: St. Anthony, St. Joseph, and a statue of the Virgin Mary holding a baby Jesus. A harvest wreath, undoubtedly blessed the previous autumn, hung on one wall; a crucifix hung opposite it.

Stefan's young wife led the Szumkowskis through one of the three doors that led to the other rooms. "This is where you'll be staying."

Tosh, Ronka, and Trina stood crowded in the doorway. This room, like the kitchen, was white-washed and decorated with brilliant *wycinanki.* There was one bed, covered with a straw mattress. Atop the mattress lay a coarse bleached sheet, neatly folded; a huge feather pillow; and a *pierzyna,* a plump feather tick. The room also contained a washstand with a china bowl, a small table with a vase containing dried flowers, and two wooden stools. Hooks to hold clothing had been driven into the walls.

"Thank you," said Ronka. "This is very nice."

Tosh hurried back outside to unload the family's belongings. While he and Ronka decided where to stow their possessions, Trina sat watching, hugging her rag doll.

The bedroom door had been left open to admit heat from the kitchen. The Szumkowskis would learn that the stove was the only regular source of heat in the winter.

Just as Ronka and Tosh were completing their tidying up, Stefan's wife appeared in the doorway. "We eat now. Come."

The Szumkowskis filed back into the kitchen and sat down on one of the long benches. Stefan had taken his place at the head of the table. An old woman sat in the other carved chair at the foot. The two girls who had been introduced as Stefan's sisters began helping his wife set food on the table. When everything had been placed to their satisfaction, the young women sat down on the remaining bench. The *babusia* crossed herself, bent her head, and began saying a prayer. The others joined in. When the prayer had ended, Stefan picked up the nearest bowl, served himself, and passed the bowl to Tosh. Soon everyone was busy eating.

Trina could hardly believe her eyes. There were boiled potatoes topped with crumbled bacon and fried onions, great slabs of well-buttered bread, and bowlsful of thick *polewina,* a buttermilk soup. It was a typical farmhouse meal, but to the Szumkowskis, fresh from the Poznań camp, it seemed like a feast.

As they ate, the two families stole quick looks at each other. Finally Ronka broke the silence. "We are the Szumkowskis," she said to the women. "My husband's name is Tosh, mine is Ronka, and this is our little girl, Trina."

Stefan looked up from his bowl. "Our family name is Nowakowski," he said, and, nodding toward his wife: "Zosia." Nodding at his sisters, he continued, "Marysia and Józia." Then, pointing to the old woman: "My mother's mother, my grandmother."

When the meal was over the young women stood up and began clearing the table. Ronka got up to help them. Stefan rolled himself a cigarette, and then offered the little sack of tobacco and a sheaf of thin papers to Tosh. Tosh shook his head. "Thank you, I don't smoke."

After the dishes had been placed in the tub, Marysia, who looked like the elder of the two sisters, sprinkled water on the beaten earth floor. When she had swept the floor thoroughly, she covered it with fresh sawdust. Meanwhile, her sister and sister-in-law, helped by Ronka, did the dishes. The old woman, wrapped in a huge woolen shawl, had moved to the oven ledge, where she sat nodding. Soon Stefan got up, put on his coat, and went outside to the barn to do chores.

The young women, finished with housework, set out baskets of goose feathers. Backs to the table, they settled down on the floor and, handful by handful, began stripping the fuzz from the feathered quills.

"We'll make a *pierzyna* out of these," Zosia explained. She extended a handful of feathers to Ronka. "Like to try?"

The four women sat in companionable silence, working. The old *baba* dozed in her corner. Outside, the sky darkened. . . .

5

March dragged on interminably. The Siberian winds
blew. More snow fell. Wolves howled in the distance,
sounding closer and closer every day. The little village of Warznica virtually disappeared under snowdrifts. People plodded from house to barn, seldom
venturing out except to do their chores and answer
calls of nature.

Tosh and Ronka were anxious to repay the Nowakowskis for their food and lodging. But how? Ronka
helped all she could with the household chores, but
in the wintertime, with no garden to tend, no preserves to put up, no mushrooms to gather and dry,
there was little for the women to do. In the summertime there would be frantic activity, but for now
their work was limited to feathers and sewing.

Tosh, too, felt at a loss. He knew nothing about farm work or animals—he joked that he couldn't tell the backside of a cow from its front. There were four other families from the Poznań camp in Warznica, and they, too, seemed unable to find ways to help out their hosts. Some chafed at their inactivity; others took advantage of it and loafed unashamedly.

For Tosh, the problem of enforced idleness resolved itself unexpectedly. A few weeks after their arrival in Warznica, there was a flurry of excitement when a buggy drove into town. It pulled up at the manor house and its driver, a small, sharp-eyed man dressed in city clothes, stepped down. The owner of the *dwór* and his wife joined the visitor on the stoop; then they all went inside.

Soon a wagon set out from the *dwór*. It stopped at every house in the village, and each time its driver got out. Before long everyone knew why the official had come. Each of the villagers was to prepare a list of his personal holdings. Every pig must be accounted for; each cow listed, along with her estimated milk yield. All the fields were to be described in terms of crops planted and harvests expected. The peasants spoke respectfully of the official's "papers," but showed a country people's typical distrust of anything and anyone strange—an attitude strengthened by the fact that this stranger was clearly hand-in-glove with the Germans.

When the official drew up at the Nowakowskis'

door, Tosh saw a chance to be useful. "Would you like me to read the documents to you?" he asked Stefan.

The farmer nodded. Tosh threw on his hat and coat and hurried outside. After a discussion with the Germans' emissary he came back clutching a sheaf of papers. He was followed by virtually every man living in the village.

In the warmth of Stefan's kitchen, Tosh read slowly and clearly from the "papers." From time to time he paused to discuss a word or phrase. Not only did the Germans demand an inventory (a word strange to the villagers), they were imposing a quota, Tosh explained. If a farmer raised forty bushels of potatoes, he was to deliver thirty to the Germans. If one of his pigs had a litter of six, he would be permitted to keep just one piglet. In the future all orders would be posted at the nearest town, and it would be the peasants' responsibility to read and obey them. Disobedience would be punished by prison terms, and failure to deliver a quota could mean death.

The farmers were clearly worried. It was the usually taciturn Stefan who finally stated what bothered them most. "We don't know our letters. How can we find out what the Germans want?"

"Would you like me to teach you to read?" Tosh asked.

"I'm too old," came a voice from the crowd.

40

"The priest tried to teach me once. Couldn't," another farmer chimed in.

Again it was Stefan who was heard above the hubbub. "We will meet here in my house. *Pan* Tosh will teach."

And so it was decided.

The following day Tosh asked Stefan for the wagon. His first stop was at the *dwór*. After a brief conversation with the owner, he turned the wagon around and set out for the town in which he and Ronka and Trina had disembarked from the train.

After some searching, Tosh found the small house he was looking for. At his knock, the door opened a crack, and a little old lady peered out. It took some time for Tosh to convince her that it was safe to let him in. "*Pan* Krysztofer sent me. He told me that you could help me. I need books. Books and paper. I don't suppose you would have a child's blackboard, would you?"

The old woman scrutinized Tosh in silence. "Hmm . . ." she muttered at last. "I suppose if Krysztofer says I can trust you, it's all right. Let's go over to the schoolhouse and see what we can find."

Soon two bundled-up figures were making their way to the town's central square. From the outside, the schoolhouse resembled the houses around it, with its thatched roof and whitewashed facade. But inside, there were differences. The floors were wooden, and the rooms were equipped with electricity.

The old woman gripped Tosh by the shoulder. "Did you know that next month *they* are going to come in here to go through all the books?" She snorted. "We can't use the library until the 'undesirable' books are removed. I can just imagine what *they* will consider undesirable."

Tosh's eyes widened as the old schoolteacher unlocked the door to an inner room. "Ah! Here we are. Take your pick. You will need the primers, of course . . . and the history books . . . and Mickiewicz, Sienkiewicz, Zamyski. . . . But be selective. We have to have something left for the *Szwabs* to burn!"

For a while the two worked silently in the chilly room. They studied the books one by one. Some they set aside, others they dismissed with a glance. At last they paused, satisfied with their selections. The schoolteacher led Tosh to a small closet.

"Now let's see what we have in the way of paper and pencils. Not much, I'm afraid. We don't have a portable blackboard, either, but then you don't really need one. You can use the floor. With little scuffing you'll have a fine writing surface."

When Tosh had loaded everything he needed into the wagon, he clasped the old woman's hand. "Thank you, professor. I'll give you a progress report from time to time."

"Thank *you, Pan* Tosh. It is such a pity—such minds that go to waste—but every child is a pair of hands, and they are needed as soon as the child can walk. The littlest tend geese, the older ones look after cows. By the time they are fourteen or fifteen they can run a farm single-handed. Still . . ."

Tosh got into the wagon and flicked the reins, giving the animal its head. The horse knew the way back to his hay and oats. He trotted along briskly.

And so the classes started. In the afternoons, after the chores were done, a dozen or so young men congregated in the Nowakowskis' kitchen. There were a few women as well, including Stefan's sisters, Zosia, Trina and two young girls from the Poznań barracks also sat in on the lessons. Stefan and his wife quickly outdistanced the other villagers. It wasn't very long before both were reading simple books by themselves.

Ronka's turn to prove herself useful came a bit later. It all began one night when the foehn, a warm wind from the south, began blowing, bringing a sudden thaw. By morning melting snow had turned the road into a river and the farmyard into a lake. That noon, Zosia's labor pains began. Consternation reigned. How could the midwife be summoned? The roads were totally impassable.

Ronka took charge. Not for nothing was she the

daughter of a *dziad,* a medicine man. Many was the time she had watched her father bring a new life into the world. She quickly sent Marysia and Józia off to the well for water, and told Stefan to build a roaring fire in the kitchen stove. She used homespun linen to line one of the oval baskets usually used for fruit picking; then she rolled up her sleeves. Everyone except Stefan's sisters was shooed from the room. Stefan's son, a blonde, blue-eyed baby, as fair as his two parents, was born before sundown.

Zosia was full of praise for the city woman. Ronka became little Toshek's godmother, and from then on had all the work she could handle. Pregnant women, ailing babies, and children with broken bones, filled the Nowakowskis' kitchen to bursting. Ronka was consulted about infected fingers . . . cradle cap on babies' scalps . . . and she was even asked to deliver calves, the ultimate tribute from peasants, who valued livestock above all else. Though money was scarce and its value uncertain, Ronka was well paid in chickens, eggs, butter, and other victuals.

6

With the coming of spring the countryside burst into bloom. There were yellow buttercups and blue forget-me-nots on the banks of the streams, pink and white blossoms on the cherry and apple trees, golden catkins on the birches, and new green everywhere.

The village became a whirlwind of activity. There was plowing, sowing, planting to be done. Women scurried about setting hens on eggs. Children led cows up to the summer pastures. Attendance at Tosh's classes dwindled dramatically.

As soon as the yard had dried out a little, Stefan climbed up to the thatched roof of the barn carrying a large wagon wheel. When he had fixed the wooden round securely in place on the roof, the girls gathered armloads of dry twigs and placed them enticingly near the barn. During the days that followed, the Nowakowskis anxiously scanned the skies to the south. Would they come? Would they pick this household, when so many other rooftops in the village had been prepared with equal care?

One morning the usually impassive Stefan burst into the house. "They're here!" he shouted. "They're here! The storks have arrived!"

Everyone dropped what they were doing and ran outside. Two huge birds were gliding in ever-narrowing circles over the Nowakowski house. Around and around they flew before finally perching on the barn, where they stood clicking and clacking their bills, for all the world like a husband and wife arguing over the merits of a new house. For what seemed like an eternity, the entire Nowakowski family stood silently watching the two great birds. At last one of the storks flexed its majestic wings and sailed down into the yard. There, with long-legged dignified strides, looking like a caricature of a college professor, it walked over to the twig pile. After more bill clacking, it picked up a twig and returned to the roof.

The Nowakowskis sighed in unison. Then Stefan stepped forward, bowed formally to the birds, and, cap in hand, introduced his family to the storks. Each family member bowed to the birds. Then they all returned to the house. Stefan brought out a bottle of vodka and passed drinks all around. Good crops and good health were insured for the coming year. The storks were here!

Trina would always remember that spring and summer as the happiest time of her life. Ronka was perpetually busy, but Tosh, with his classes at a virtual standstill, had a good deal of time on his hands. The village children, involved in their summer work, were not available to play with Trina. So Trina and Tosh roamed the countryside together.

Sometimes they would lie on their backs in the middle of a meadow, Tosh with a long stem of grass between his teeth, Trina with an even longer one, listening to the meadowlark. Together they got up in the middle of the night to sit under the lilac bush and listen to the nightingale. They walked in the woods and learned to navigate by the stars and the moss. Once they followed the owl on his silent midnight prowls and watched him scoop up a rabbit in his claws.

Often, as they sat in a forest glade or watched the busy comings and goings of the ants, Tosh told Trina stories: of Wanda, the flaxen-haired warrior queen who, when vanquished by a German prince, chose death under the waves of the Warta River rather than marry him; of Great-grandfather Antoine, a general in Napoleon's army who loved Poland so much he changed his name to Antek and never returned to France; of knights in gold armor and their white horses who sleep inside a hollow Tatra mountain and wait.

"What are they waiting for?"

"For Poland to need them. Then they will awake and ride out into battle to free their country."

"Why don't they wake up now, and chase the *Szwabs* out?"

"Trina," Tosh said slowly, "do you know what a myth is?"

"You mean the knights aren't real?" Trina asked with disappointment.

"They're real in a way," Tosh replied. And, seeing the puzzled look on Trina's face, he continued, "The sleeping knights are waiting for the right time to strike—they're all of us, Trina, all of the Polish people. Each one of us is a knight, and when the time comes, we'll fight."

As summer drew to an end, Tosh began making occasional forays into nearby towns and cities, trying to find work. He had not had much luck. Since there were no openings for lawyers now that the Germans had imposed their own brand of law, Tosh was forced to range farther and farther in his search. In mid-October, he found a position in Radom, a small city about two hundred kilometers from Warznica, as a translator for the *Sondergericht.* This was the special court set up by the Germans to try cases of treason and insubordination. Tosh also found a place in Radom for the family to live.

The Szumkowskis packed their small bundles once again and prepared to leave Warznica. The entire village gathered to say good-bye. Tears were shed. Every family had a present for Ronka, and they pressed forward to hand her their gifts: geese with their feet bound . . . a hand-carved water dipper . . . a square of homespun cloth.

Stefan drove them to the train in the same wagon that had brought them to the village. When they arrived at the railroad stop, Trina and her parents unloaded their bundles and settled down to wait. Train schedules were erratic, in spite of German efficiency, and they were prepared for a delay.

At last a long whistle echoed along the track. As the train pulled up, the Szumkowskis said their last good-byes to Stefan. Then they climbed aboard. They were on their way to Radom.

7

The lodgings Tosh had found for his family were located directly behind the building housing the *Sondergericht,* in a sprawling apartment complex built around a *podwórko,* a large open courtyard. The *podwórko* contained a huge gnarled wild pear tree, a huddle of sheds used by the tenants to house assorted poultry, and a square of grass. A huge warren of basements lay below, a many-corridored maze connecting with other basements and extending under most of the city.

The Szumkowskis' new home was part of a three-room apartment. Two of the rooms were already occupied by a Jewish family, the Krols. Tosh, Ronka, and Trina moved into the kitchen, a long, narrow room containing an impressive range with tiled sides, and a sink. Given the desperate housing conditions in Radom, they considered themselves very lucky.

All the traffic in the apartment had to pass through the kitchen, so the very first thing Ronka did was to string a clothesline upon which she hung sheets, creating a screened corner where they would have some privacy. While she unpacked, Tosh hurried off to the marketplace to buy a straw mattress. By nightfall he had fashioned a rough bedstead and had hung shelves for their few pots and dishes. Trina worked with him, driving in nails on which they would hang their clothes. The next day Ronka managed to scrounge a table and three chairs, and their household was complete.

Trina immediately began exploring her new surroundings. She quickly discovered children of her own age in the neighborhood. Directly behind their apartment lived a tall blonde boy just a few years older than she. His name was Janek, and he owned all of Jules Verne's books. Across the courtyard lived a girl almost exactly her age named Nina. No two girls could have looked more unlike. Trina had grown almost painfully thin, while Nina was stocky and broad-shouldered. Trina wore her brown hair in thin braids down her back; Nina's thick blonde hair was cropped as short as a boy's. Trina's eyes were brown, Nina's blue. Their personalities were equally different: Trina was shy and quiet, prefering to keep to herself; Nina was loud and boisterous, given to fistfights with the boys. Yet the two girls became fast friends.

Nina's mother, Janina, was built on the same generous scale as her daughter. Like Tosh, she worked at the court. Shortly after Tosh began working for the *Sondergericht,* Janina came calling. Ronka shooed Trina out to play with Nina, and the three adults closeted themselves in the kitchen. They talked for hours. Trina, playing under the open window, could hear only disjointed phrases that seemed to make no sense:

"It's dangerous . . . think of . . ."

"I am thinking . . . all those people . . . lives . . ."

"What if you get caught?"

"Somebody has . . . I will *not* get caught . . . risk in everyday . . ."

Only much later did Trina realize what the conversation had been about. As it turned out, Tosh began working for the underground, the *Andrzejki,* that very day. At the time, Trina had no idea that she, too, would become part of the Resistance. Ronka, fearful for Tosh's life, disapproved of Tosh's involvement with the partisans, but she didn't stand in his way. She was not to find out about Trina for a long, long time.

The Szumkowskis soon became fast friends with their new neighbors, Mojszek and Hanna Krol. Mojszek ran a busy tailoring business. His sister Rebeka and Hanna's brother David also lived in the apartment complex. The Krols had two rooms to themselves, the larger one served as the *warsztat,* the workshop. Mojszek could have passed for a Gentile—he was tall, blue-eyed, and blonde, a true Nordic type. But when he spoke he gave himself away instantly—the accent was pure Yiddish. Hanna, on the other hand, spoke flawless Polish, but her looks reflected her ancestry.

Despite the uncertainty of their existence during a period when rumors flew about the establishment of a ghetto, the Krols were happy, cheerful people, busy all day long. Hanna, who was childless, concerned herself greatly with Trina's welfare and kept cooking her special dishes. "The child is entirely too thin," she'd say. "I just made some carrot *tzimes.* Send Trina over."

Or, "I have some nice stuffed *derma,* Ronka."

Or, "Tell Trina to drop by. There's sour cream and herring today."

Despite all she ate, Trina stayed as thin as a rail. But that didn't discourage Hanna. She simply shook her head and redoubled her efforts.

Mojszek was just as concerned about Trina in his way. He decided that something must be done about her threadbare wardrobe. Rummaging

53

through piles of scraps, he'd mutter, "Nu, not enough here," or, "Nice piece goods, this. Hmm, give the *goyim* a little less collar, shorter hem. . . ." And he'd save a piece here and a piece there until, by Christmas, he'd saved enough cloth to make Trina a coat with a real fur collar and a peaked cap to match. He also made her a *mundurek,* the kind of sailor outfit that every schoolgirl had worn before the war. The hem and the seams were so deep that Trina was able to wear it for years to come.

In January, two important events took place in the Krols' lives. Mojszek's sister and Hanna's brother got married, and Hanna learned that she was pregnant.

The wedding was held in the *warsztat,* tidied up and bedecked for the occasion with paper streamers. Hanna made tons of food. There was music and dancing. Trina was enthralled by the bearded rabbi and the traditional canopy beneath which the couple were married. The symbolic smashing of the wineglass at the end of the ceremony fascinated her.

The wedding took place in the third week of January, 1941. In the second week of February, not long before Trina's ninth birthday, the Germans announced the formation of the Radom ghetto. Its boundaries were marked off, and everyone living within them was told to move out. Walls were erected to bar exits and entrances to the restricted area; the only access would be through guarded gates. Lists were posted in public places telling Jews when to move into the ghetto, and where.

One by one the Jewish families in Radom disappeared behind the walls. A few chose not to go, but to hide or run instead. This caused immediate announcements over the strategically located street-corner loudspeakers warning that the penalty for hiding a Jew was death. Despite this proclamation, an underground network sprang up. People with access to records erased recent births. Death certificates were forged, especially for young children of Aryan appearance.

The day finally came when it was the Krols' turn to go. Tosh, who had "pull" through his job, immediately arranged for passes that would enable Hanna and Mojszek to get out of the ghetto on errands, and passes for himself and Trina that would get them in. Ronka, the ever-practical one, persuaded Tosh to apply at once for the big room and permission was granted for the Szumkowskis to move into the former *warsztat.* A chemical engineer named Zymski was assigned to the small middle room of the apartment, and the kitchen was assigned to both of the tenants jointly.

The Krols moved into one room of an ancient building abutting one of the newly erected ghetto walls. The walls were crumbling, and the only existing plumbing was on the staircase. Still, they considered themselves fortunate, because they could see the park from their only window. They particularly enjoyed the view because the park was *Verboten,* forbidden, to everyone—Jews and Poles alike—but the Germans!

In late August, 1941, Hanna gave birth to a boy and promptly named him David. Tosh, notified of the event by one of the countless runners from the *Andrzejki,* went into action. Three days after David's birth he went to the ghetto wearing his best suit, his pants pressed into painfully sharp creases. In the basket he carried were uniforms; a vial of poppy extract; a carefully concealed death certificate for one male infant of Jewish race, stillborn; and a birth certificate made out in the names of Maryja and Stanislaw Kowalski, parents. After making sure that the guard at the gate was one who did not know him, Tosh walked boldly up to the entranceway.

"I have no time to spend chattering with underlings. Out of the way!" And with that Tosh marched through the gate. He could feel the guard's eyes on his back, but kept on walking rapidly, certain that his unruffled manner and accentless speech would deceive the guard, who would think that only another German could act with such authority. He was right. There was no order to stop, no shouted "Halt!"

But when Tosh arrived at the Krols' dilapidated

building, he was greeted by silence. Open doors creaked on their hinges. Wind blew papers about. Only yesterday it had been a teeming warren of humanity—today it stood still and empty.

Tosh, who knew without asking what had happened, felt he must ask all the same. But the people from neighboring buildings edged away when he approached them. Finally one bearded old man stepped forward.

"This man is a friend," he said to the others. "Come, we talk."

They sat in the dank little closet that the old man called home. "They came yesterday," he said, "about noon. With trucks—Hoffman's men and soldiers. They drove everybody outside." The old man paused. "You know Hoffman?" he asked.

"I know Hoffman," Tosh acknowledged.

"Hoffman stood right in the middle of the courtyard smacking that whip he carries against his boots. They lined everybody up. Men on one side. Women on the other. I was watching from the window on the staircase. Out there—" The old man pointed. "Then they went through the lines. Old people, children, one way; good strong men, women . . ." The old man's voice faltered. "Hanna, she tried to keep the baby. Soldier grabbed it . . . she hit the soldier. Hoffman . . . he took the baby. He smiled at Hanna. Called her over. When Hanna ran toward him he swung the baby. Cracked his head on the wall. Hanna screamed. Tried to scratch Hoffman. The pig laughed. Then he shot her."

Trina lay in bed, her face to the wall. She listened to Tosh and Ronka talking. On the wall above the bed hung the coat Mojszek had made for her. She lay very still, her teeth pressed into the flesh of her hand. Although she had bitten through the skin, she felt no pain.

"One goddamned day too late . . . one day . . . ," Tosh muttered.

"I'm going to have a mass said for Hanna and the baby. I'm sure their Jehovah wouldn't mind a Catholic prayer. What about Mojszek? Did the man . . . ?"

"Ziemczak, the old man, he said he thought Mojszek had been put in the labor group. I'm going to find out what I can."

"Who . . . ?"

"Hoffman." Tosh's voice was grim. "I'll let the *Andrzejki* know. They'll set up a tribunal."

Trina struggled awake. A hand covered her mouth. "Shh . . . don't talk. Get dressed." Tosh whispered. "Get your things on and then come outside."

Trina pulled her clothes on in total darkness. The heavy blackout curtain had been drawn across the windows at the first sign of dusk, and now there was not even a glimmer of light. Following Tosh's instructions, she slipped through Zymski's room and into the kitchen. She heard a faint creak as Tosh opened the hallway door. She followed her father downstairs to the basement entrance. It was not until the heavy wooden door had clicked behind them that Tosh lit a candle.

"Come with me, Trina," he said. "There is something we must do." They threaded their way through a maze of shadowy cubicles. "Memorize the way, Trina," Tosh whispered. "It's very important."

"*Dobrze,* very well," she answered. "I'll remember."

At last they stopped by a wall. Tosh dripped wax on the floor and set the candle into it. "Look," he said. "See this brick?"

Trina nodded.

"See how it's chipped here? Now watch." As Tosh pressed the worn place, the brick slid aside, revealing a hollow space. There were bundles wrapped in oilcloth inside.

"Now listen carefully, Trina." Tosh stooped down until his eyes were level with Trina's. "Someday this war will end, and justice will be done. But our side will need evidence—names, dates, places. Remember this place. If anything happens to me, see that the right people get these papers. Promise?"

Trina nodded. "I promise."

Tosh slid the brick back. No trace of the hiding place remained. Trina followed her father back to their living quarters and crept into bed, but she didn't sleep another wink that night.

8

A faint line of gray was showing at the edge of the blackout curtain when Trina got up. She pulled on her clothes and noiselessly slipped through the engineer's room. In the kitchen she paused long enough to tuck a heel of dark, hard bread into her pocket, to wash her face and hands in cold water, and to plait her hair without the help of a mirror. Then she hurried out the door.

She stood in the courtyard looking at the window of Nina's room. The curtains were still tightly drawn. She sat on the doorstep for a while, scuffing the concrete with the toes of her wooden-soled shoes. It was a hazy morning. Even the rising sun could not dispel the fog. Trina pulled out the chunk of bread and munched it slowly. Finally she got up, picked up a small stone, and threw it at Nina's window. She waited, then tossed another pebble. The curtains behind the glass moved. Nina's face appeared briefly; then the dark cloth fell back into place. Trina settled back on the doorstep to wait. She did not have to wait long.

"Did you hear about the Krols?" Trina asked Nina.

Nina nodded.

"Tosh says Hoffman did it."

"Hoffman?"

"The Gestapo officer."

"Where can we find him, Trina?"

"He works at the *Szwab* headquarters across from St. Pawet's church."

For a while the girls sat in silence on the doorstep.

"Think the curfew is up yet?" Nina finally asked.

Trina studied the sun. "It looks like it to me," she answered.

"Let's go."

The two girls got up, dusted themselves off, and headed toward the *brama,* the large entranceway to the apartment complex. The *brama* was wide enough to admit a wagon and ran the entire width of the building. The concierge's apartment opened off it so that he could watch the tenants' comings and goings. Opposite his windows lay the staircase to the upper floors. Massive wooden portals shut the *brama* at night; a smaller door cut into the portals admitted latecomers, who either carried keys or pounded on the door until the concierge let them in.

As the girls approached the *brama,* the concierge was just unlocking the smaller door. He paid no heed to them; he was used to the odd hours they kept. The girls made their way to Zeromska Street. There they turned left and continued walking until they reached a small church surrounded by well-tended grounds. Huge chestnut trees shaded the churchyard walks. A few unripened chestnuts lay on the ground, their green, spiny husks split open. The girls headed for a bench facing a certain building across the street from the church.

"Do you know what he looks like?" Nina asked.

"Yes—I know," Trina said. "Sometimes I take Tosh's lunch up to him when he has a lot of work. I see Hoffman there. He comes to the trials—he's there all the time. He's tall. Taller than Tosh. He wears glasses. The kind without rims. I'd know him anywhere."

The two girls settled on the bench. They picked a few chestnuts off the ground. Nina began stringing hers into a necklace while Trina tried to carve out a miniature basket. From time to time signs of activity outside the building across the street caused the girls to look up from their play. On each occasion,

Trina shook her head; *No, he's not the one,* she signaled.

The girls continued to gather chestnuts. When they had cleared the ground around the bench, they threw rocks into the branches to knock down more of the green fruit. After Nina had finished two necklaces and Trina had carved a dozen little baskets, a motorcycle pulled up to the curb across the street. Trina nudged Nina. "That's him," she said. "The tall thin one."

Nina pulled a ball from her pocket and began bouncing it. After a few bounces she let the ball get away. It rolled off the curb and into the road. Nina ran after it. As she stooped to retrieve it, she peered at the German from under her lowered eyelids. Finally she picked up the ball and skipped back to where Trina was sitting.

"I'll remember him. What do we do now?" she asked Trina.

"We'll need help. We have to find out what he does every day. . . ." Trina's voice trailed off. "Who do you think we can trust?"

"Janek," Nina said firmly, "Janek, and maybe Roman, the carpenter's son. Janek had a brother who got killed at the front. And Roman's sister—something terrible happened to her. I don't know quite what, but it had something to do with the Germans. And what about Kasia? Do you think she'd be all right? You know—the one who lives in the back with her grandmother. Her folks were arrested and nobody's seen them—" Nina broke off at the puzzled look on Trina's face. "You *know, Kasia.* She never talks to anybody, just sits on her stoop. And Jurek, perhaps. No, he talks too much."

"Janek, yes," Trina answered quickly. "Kasia? I guess we can count on her. You're right about Jurek, though. He talks too much. All right, let's go and have a word with them."

Back home, they made the rounds of the courtyard.

"Is Janek home?" they asked at one door. "Can he come out and play?"

Janek joined them. Once they were out of earshot, he looked from Nina to Trina and asked, "What's all this about? You've never come calling for me before! What's up?"

"Just come with us. We'll explain when we've collected the others," Trina answered.

They made their way to the carpentry shop at the back of the courtyard and asked for Roman. He seemed as surprised and suspicious as Janek. The four children then moved on to a creaky old building at the rear of the complex where they collected Kasia. When all five children were assembled, Nina pointed to the poultry sheds. "That way," she said. "We can talk there without anybody hearing."

When they had settled down on a pile of old sacks amidst the roosting chickens, Nina broke the silence.

"Now," she said to Trina, "tell them what happened to the Krols."

Trina related what she had overheard the previous night. "Nina and I have seen the man who killed Hanna and the baby," she concluded. "Are you with us?"

"I am," responded Janek. "Mojszek gave me my first pair of long pants."

"Me too," Roman answered firmly. "Hanna nursed my sister when—Me too," he repeated. "Me too."

"You can count me in," Kasia added. "Hanna sent food over when my *babusia* was sick. And gave me a sweater, and— Count me in."

For the next two weeks, five small shadows trailed the Gestapo officer morning and night. They found out where he was billeted, what time he left each morning to go to headquarters, when he returned home, what route he routinely traveled. Soon they could predict his every move.

They held a second meeting in the poultry shed. This time Janek spoke first. "Every morning about six he goes for a long walk in the park. He circles it five times. I'm sure the best place to do our job is by the old castle ruins. There are so many bushes there that you can't see a thing, and if we pick a foggy or rainy morning, there won't be a soul around."

"How do we get into the park?" Kasia asked. "It's

off limits. We could never get past the entrance."

"Use your head. We don't need to go near the gate. One side of the park gives onto courtyards. We can climb in from there, over the fence."

"What about the curfew?" asked Trina. "How can we get to the park early enough in the morning?"

"We'll just have to be there the night before," Janek answered. "Tell your parents you're spending the night with a friend. That way—"

Roman interrupted. "I know how to get to the park through the basements and sewers."

"The sewers are no good," Janek said firmly. "They've been mining them."

"Janek's right," Nina interjected. "We'll have to start out the night before and wait."

"We'll meet here every day until we decide the time is right," Janek said. "The first evening it rains, we'll go."

The next few days were sunny and cloudless. The group met in the shed morning and evening, disturbing the chickens. They filled socks with wet sand. They honed knives. They discussed their practice runs to the area surrounding the park and compared routes. One day Janek brought a piece of paper with him. He unfolded it and passed it from hand to hand. "We'll pin this on him," he announced.

In beautifully scripted letters, the paper read:

JOHANN HOFFMAN
MORDERCA
WERDYKT: WINNY
WYROK: SMIERĆ
USKUTECZNIONE PRZEZ: SZARYCH RYCERZY

JOHANN HOFFMAN
MURDERER
VERDICT: GUILTY
SENTENCE: DEATH
EXECUTED BY: THE GRAY KNIGHTS

"That's what we'll call ourselves," Janek said. "The Gray Knights." Trina shivered, remembering Tosh's words. It was just as he'd said, "every Pole is a knight . . ." And now the time had come for them to fight.

At last a day dawned dark and gloomy, with the promise of rain by nightfall. Each child got permission from a parent, or in Kasia's case a grandparent, to spend the night with a friend. That afternoon they met briefly in the shed and solemnly shook hands all around.

"See you in the castle ruins," said Janek.

"In the ruins," echoed the others.

Trina and Nina set out from their *podwórko* looking like any two girls engaged in chasing a ball down the street. They bounced it, and caught it, and let it fall away until the chase finally brought them within sight of the park. Then they stopped and bounced the ball back and forth until it rolled into the entranceway of an apartment complex adjoining the park. They hurried after the ball into an empty courtyard.

By now, it was dusk and a fine rain was falling. The girls scanned the windows. They were covered with blackout curtains. "What do we do now?" Nina whispered, even though there was no one to overhear them.

"We'll wait here until it gets really dark and the park has been closed for the night. It shouldn't be long," Trina answered. "Let's see if there's someplace to hide."

They investigated the courtyard. This *podwórko*, unlike their own, had no sheds in which they might conceal themselves.

"What about the garbage bin?" Nina suggested.

Trina shivered. "Somebody might dump slops on us. And there are rats in there!"

Nina shuddered. "Look," she hissed.

Nina pointed to an open trapdoor leading to the coal bins. The girls walked over and peered into the opening. In the gathering darkness it was nearly impossible to see into the cellar.

"What if we can't climb back out?" asked Trina. "I think we'd better just stay out here. Who's going to come snooping around this late, especially in the rain?"

They circled the courtyard again, and found a niche in the wall where two buildings met. This offered protection of a sort, and they settled down on the damp concrete to wait.

"Want some *machorka?*" Nina asked, producing a little sack of tobacco and some papers. After they had rolled cigarettes in the darkness, Nina fished in the depths of her clothing and came up with a match. She struck it against the wall. The acrid smell of smoke drifted about their heads as they dragged on their crudely rolled cigarettes.

The minutes seemed to crawl by. But at last it was time to move on. The girls got up stiffly and walked to the back of the courtyard, which abutted the park. They stopped in front of a high iron fence decorated with ornamental scrolls and topped with spikes.

"I think I can squeeze between the railings, Nina," Trina whispered.

"But how are you going to get in?"

"Climb over. You go first and wait on the other side so you can help me if I get stuck on top."

Trina poked her head through the railings to be sure it would pass, then withdrew it. Turning her body sideways, she carefully wiggled between the cold iron bars. Nina then placed a foot on one of the ornamental scrolls, and with a hop managed to grasp the top of the fence. Pulling herself up, she threw a leg over between two spikes. She balanced herself briefly at the top, and jumped. They were in.

The two girls walked stealthily through the trees, emerging only to dart quickly across an occasional pathway. At last they arrived at the ruins.

"Psst . . ." A whisper floated out of the darkness. Janek was already there, waiting.

"Where are Roman and Kasia?"

"Not here yet. Sit down and try to relax."

The children waited, safely hidden behind the thick walls of the ruins. Nina rolled more cigarettes. They smoked.

Suddenly Janek stiffened. "Someone's coming," he whispered.

It was Kasia. Roman followed shortly. The conspirators reviewed their strategy one last time. Then they settled back to wait. The clock on the church tower at the back of the park marked off the hours. *Bong, bong, bong. . . .*

When the clock struck five, they assumed their assigned positions. Roman and Janek climbed a tree on opposite sides of the path. Stretched out on the thick branches, the boys were invisible from below. The girls crouched in the undergrowth that bordered the walkway. There was nothing to do now but wait. The minutes dragged on forever.

Footsteps at last! A ramrod-straight figure

marched by. They let him pass, and gazed in silence at his retreating back. Again approaching footsteps . . . once more they let him pass. When the officer appeared for the third time, Janek and Roman dropped from the trees like cats.

"Whaa . . . ?" Whatever Hoffman was going to say remained unfinished. The sand-packed sock connected solidly with his head. The girls sprang from the underbrush, and they bound Hoffman securely with the ropes they had carried tied about their waists. Trina shoved a rag into his mouth. They dragged the officer to the ruins; then the girls scuffed up the path and carefully spread leaves over the matted foliage.

"We'll wait until he comes to," Janek whispered. "He must know why."

They did not have to wait long. Within minutes Hoffman had stirred and opened his eyes. He stared at the children. His look of comprehension was quickly followed by one of rage. The SS officer struggled against his bonds, but the girls had done their job well.

The five young conspirators formed a circle. Their faces were solemn. Janek stepped forward and spoke:

"Johann Hoffman, you have been charged with the murder of Hanna and David Krol, and you have been found guilty. We therefore sentence you to death. We will carry out the sentence now."

Janek swiftly bent down and pulled the dagger from the sheath at Hoffman's belt. The two boys flipped the German over onto his stomach. Then Janek took a handful of Hoffman's hair and lifted his head. With his other hand he made a quick slash across the officer's throat. One by one the others took the dagger and repeated Janek's gesture.

Finally they turned the German over again, face up. Janek pinned the prepared paper to the officer's chest, then removed the gun from the holster on Hoffman's hip and tucked it into his pants. He picked up the dagger, wiped it on Hoffman's tunic and handed it to Trina. She hesitated, but then with a steady hand took the weapon and slipped it into her blouse. She looked over at Nina and noted that her friend's face was the color of dirty snow. Next to her, Kasia stood with her arms wrapped tightly about her, as if her stomach hurt. Both boys' faces were pale, their lips set in a thin line.

No one spoke.

The rain was still dripping steadily. One by one the conspirators slipped away. Trina and Nina worked their way back to the fence and into the courtyard from which they had come. The *podwórko* was still deserted. The girls hurried through it and into the street.

72

9

Trina snapped awake. She could feel beads of perspiration coursing slowly down her face. She was lying in the hollow shaped by her body in the straw mattress. Something nameless had been pursuing her across swamps and through the trees, striking out with whiplike arms. It was right behind her! Fanged and shaggy and horrible . . .

She sat up and lifted the edge of the blackout curtain. The sky was dark and clear, and she could see stars. A moon rode high in the sky. Suddenly shafts of light pierced the darkness like fingers. A wail began somewhere. There was a stirring within the room.

"What is it?" asked Tosh's sleepy voice.

Trina waited before answering. White flowers blossomed out in the crisscrossing beams of light. A staccato chattering began in the distance.

"Parachutists," Trina answered. "They're being shot down." As she watched, a flower shape crumpled and fell. She heard Tosh get up, the faint rustle of clothes as he dressed. She picked up her own clothes from beside the bed and drew them on. Tosh padded softly across the room.

"Going outside?" she asked. "Wait for me." She could hear her mother's even breathing—Ronka slept on, undisturbed. Hurriedly she put on her shoes and followed Tosh outside.

It was cool, almost nippy. Out of doors, the sounds of the distant antiaircraft guns were clearer. They sat down on the concrete doorstep and looked at the illuminated sky.

"It would be very beautiful if it weren't so horrible," Tosh said, almost to himself. "I don't suppose it matters who they are . . . Ruskis probably. We'll never know."

The small girl and the tall thin man sat side by side in companionable silence until the sky began to lighten. The searchlights had long since been extinguished and the wailing sirens hushed when they finally went back inside.

At noon Tosh came home for lunch as usual. He was breathless and uncharacteristically agitated. "Stay home today. Don't go anywhere! Anywhere!"

he insisted. "The Germans found a young Jewish boy in the next block. They haven't been able to find out who was hiding him, so they're organizing a purge. Every tenth person on the street is being picked up and arrested."

Trina hurried outside and concealed herself behind the heavy portals of the *brama*. Peeking through a crack between the hinges, she could see into the street. Men in green and black uniforms were swarming everywhere. Trucks idled at curbs. Motorcycles wove in and out of traffic. The frantic pace resembled that in an ants' nest. Trina watched for a while, ready to bolt for home at the slightest provocation. Then she went back into the courtyard to find Nina. Together the girls returned to the *brama,* drawn by the activity on the street.

It was nearly midnight before Tosh returned home, escorted by a German soldier charged with ensuring his safety. Tosh had once remarked that the only real benefit he derived from his job at the *Sondergericht* was immunity from the Germans and safe passage after hours.

He was tired and depressed. The interrogations had gone on and on—and he knew that whatever their outcome, all of the people picked up in the manhunt were condemned. Even now the work crews were erecting scaffolds in the square fronting the nearby church.

Loudspeakers boomed. Ugly words spewed forth into the morning air.

"Verrat . . . Hochverrat . . . Juden . . . Feind . . . Treason . . . high treason . . . Jews . . . the enemy . . ." The words came again and again. There was no escape from the speakers. Every street-corner post had sprouted one overnight.

At noon the next day, Tosh ignored his food. Grim-faced, he washed, shaved, brushed his clothes carefully, and shined his shoes. "Get dressed in your best," he told Ronka and Trina. "We're going to honor the dead."

The street was a sea of solemn faces. The crowd that had gathered in the brilliant late autumn sunshine was quiet and orderly. There was no pushing or shoving, no jockeying for position. Lines of men in black and green uniforms kept the townspeople back from the wooden scaffolding dominating the square. Bare wood gleamed. A forest of flaxen ropes swung in the breeze.

The crowd was dotted with enclaves of Germans— islands of noise and laughter. The Polish people edged away from the detested *Niemcy.*

A ripple ran through the crowd. They were coming. . . . No one had made an announcement, but the townspeople knew. The townspeople turned as one to watch the column come marching into the square. Hands shackled behind their backs, mouths grimly set, the prisoners advanced in an orderly fashion: men . . . women, some of them pregnant . . . a few youngsters. They walked with steady steps, their heads high.

The great doors of the church swung open. A priest dressed in magnificent gold vestments strode out bearing a monstrance. A dozen boys in scarlet surplices walked behind him. One held a huge cross; another swung an incense burner. Others bore tall burning candles.

There was a commotion among the uniformed men gathered in front of the gallows. A thin blonde officer strode angrily toward the priest. His eyebrows were in odd contrast to the blonde hair—they were dark, cutting in a straight line across his forehead. A scar slashed his right cheek.

The priest kept on walking forward until he and the German officer were face to face. The priest stood his ground, holding his monstrance chest high. The two men stared at each other for what seemed like an eternity. Then, with a shrug, the uniformed figure turned away and walked back to the viewing stand, his glasses glinting in the sun.

The column neared the gallows. One by one the condemned stepped up to the platform. One by one they put their heads through the nooses. Suddenly a voice rang out over the crowd: Father Zielinski was singing the *Requiem.* A chill passed over the crowd.

The German officer raised his hand. Trina shut

her eyes and buried her face against Tosh's body.
Steely fingers dug into her shoulders.

"*Nie* . . . no. Do not turn away. Look and remember, Trina. Don't forget . . . ever . . . ever."

They walked home without speaking, avoiding each other's eyes. Back in the square the corpses swung in the autumn breeze like macabre puppets. In the townspeoples' windows, hundreds of candles burned far into the night. The next morning the square's sidewalks were covered with flowers: purple asters, scarlet dahlias, golden chrysanthemums.

10

The bells of Swietej Katarzyny tolled mournfully for a week. The corpses continued to hang above the bright carpet of flowers, the odor of decay pronounced in the autumn air. Then, on the seventh night, an unseen crew removed the bodies. Nothing remained but a memory.

Tension grew in the city. Hoffman's body had been ferreted out by a dog being walked in the park. Another merry-go-round of investigations and interrogations was underway. Tosh was coming home later and later.

"Either it's true that nobody knows anything, or there's a hell of a good organization going," he told Ronka over a late dinner. "Not a single name has surfaced, not a clue. Nothing." He shook his head over the soup plate. "This really has the *Szwabs* puzzled. . . . I wish I could congratulate whoever did that devil Hoffman in," he continued. "It was a perfect job. What really threw *Herr* Richter into a tizzy was that verdict pinned on the body. . . . Perfect," he repeated, "perfect!"

Trina listened. Listened and fought with herself. Should she or shouldn't she? Finally she decided. That night, when the sounds of quiet breathing told her that Ronka was asleep, she crept across the room and lightly touched Tosh on the shoulder. "Can we talk?" she whispered. She sensed an answering nod. "Outside?" A second nod.

Father and daughter slipped out of the apartment like two shadows. "Tosh, I have something to show you down in the cellar. I've brought a candle."

In silence they repeated the journey of a few weeks before, when Tosh had shown Trina his hiding place. But now it was Trina who had a secret to share. She led Tosh to what had once been a wine cellar. Wine racks, laced with spider webs, held bottles with murky contents. Barrels and kegs stood in the corners.

Trina ducked behind a large barrel. When she reappeared, she was holding something. Wordlessly she stretched her hand toward Tosh. He took the object from her. Light glinted on its polished surface. Trina turned her father's hand toward the candlelight. A name was engraved on the dagger's handle: Johann Hoffman.

80

Even in the flickering light Trina could see Tosh turn pale. He groped behind him for support and sat down heavily on a cask. "Oh, *mój Boze, mój Boze,* my God, my God . . ." he whispered. "Not *you* . . ."

Trina nodded. Tosh let the dagger slip from his grasp. It lay on the brick floor, glinting. He stared blankly at the ground. Trina perched on a nearby barrel, watching him, swinging her legs. Finally Tosh lifted his head and looked Trina squarely in the eyes.

"You must never talk to *anybody else* about this. Do you understand?"

Trina nodded.

"You mustn't tell even me who was with you. I don't want to know." With a sudden flash of insight, he added, "And don't let Janina find out, either."

"How could he possibly know about Nina?" Trina wondered briefly? Then she shrugged. Tosh knew, that was all.

The Gray Knights were now meeting regularly in the shed they considered their headquarters. They gradually accumulated a number of names. Klaus Neuhauser, who had headed the manhunt . . . Carl Jenssen, the scaffold builder . . . Irma Muller . . .

"Who's Irma Muller?" Nina asked.

"An SS woman," Roman replied in a choked voice. "I watched her at the hanging. She laughed and laughed! She said, 'Look at the marionettes dance,' and she was pointing at my mother!" Roman's voice rose. "She laughed, I tell you! She laughed!"

The children exchanged glances. Irma Muller joined the list.

They began stalking again. Carefully, grimly, they set about learning all they could about their targets. They were relentless in their efforts. They breathed and dreamt revenge. They trained: they climbed fences and trees; they learned to scale walls and drainpipes. They explored rooftops and chimneys. They traveled through sewers and cellars until the rooms and passages under the city became as familiar as their own courtyard.

November 11 arrived—the anniversary of countless Polish revolutions. Before dawn the conspirators met in a cemetery at the edge of town. Each carried a flag marked with a broken cross. After building a bonfire, they consigned the flags to the flames. As the flames danced before them, they slashed their fingers and mingled their blood together, swearing eternal friendship and brotherhood.

Afterward, they sat around the fire roasting potatoes poached from a nearby field.

"I wish we could do something *really* big," Janek said, staring into the fire. "Something colossal."

"What if—" Kasia began, but then she shook her head. "No . . ."

"What?" the others asked eagerly. "What?"

"I was going to say, what if we blew up a train?

A munitions train? Listen, maybe it's possible. My uncle Franek works in the switchyards. I've seen him switch trains—it's not hard," she said, looking at the doubtful faces around her. "All you need is a long iron bar."

"We'd still have to blow it up," Roman pointed out. "Where would we get dynamite?"

"We could use gasoline," Nina broke in excitedly. "Or lamp oil."

"We *can* do it!" Janek said triumphantly, his eyes shining.

"We *can* do it," he repeated. "Kasia, find out from your uncle when the trains pass through Radom. Roman, go scout the tracks and find the best place to do it." And, turning to Nina and Trina, he said, "You two collect bottles and rags. The kind that *kvas* or vodka come in, and some rags and corks. . . . Roman, get some of the stuff your father uses to wax his caskets. That polish burns like hell. And try to find a few lengths of iron. And all of you, get lamp oil."

While their friends and families were thinking about the approaching Christmas season and how to make it festive (Ronka had immobilized a goose in an upturned kitchen stool and was force-feeding it with dumplings in order to fatten it), the fivesome scurried about the city on their own special errands. They, too, had plans for Christmas. Big plans.

———

11

All-Hallows Day was gray and wet. The candles flickering on the grave mounds were soon put out by the incessant rain. Then, sometime during the last night of November, the temperature dropped, and December arrived in a flurry of white snow and new hope. America was in war! Now the Germans were going to get it! Spirits rose again.

Borne along by the new sense of optimism, Ronka increased her efforts to create a memorable Christmas. There would be the force-fed goose; and there would be eggs donated by Tosh's clients, butter purchased on the black market, and sugar hoarded over many months for the holiday baking. Ronka secretly traded one of her coats for a gift for Trina. She even got a Christmas tree, the first they had had since the war. It was puny, to be sure, but a real live Christmas tree nonetheless, trimmed with hand-made straw decorations and beautifully painted blown eggs.

Trina couldn't wait for Christmas to come. They were ready. Everything they needed had been assembled. Kasia had learned that a big munitions transport would be passing through on December 26, St. Stefan's Day. Trina could barely conceal her excitement at the thought of the Gray Knights' Christmas present to Poland.

The Szumkowskis had guests for *vigilia,* the traditional Christmas Eve dinner. Ronka outdid herself. There was fragrant hay under the tablecloth, which had been fashioned from a sheet. The traditional even number of guests sat at the table: three Kowickis; Janina; Nina; and Nina's father, Wojciek. There was the usual empty chair and a token place setting for a stranger—the voyager who, legend claimed, was Christ traveling the earth in disguise.

There was mushroom soup, made from mushrooms gathered during the summer and early fall, and dried. There were split peas with sauerkraut; stuffed carp; and *pierogi* with cheese and more mushrooms. And, wonder of wonders, there were poppy-seed cake and honey cookies. (The fattened goose would have to wait until St. Stefan's Day, because

Christmas Eve had, since time immemorial, always been meatless.) Tosh, not to be outdone by Ronka, contributed *żubrówka,* pale green vodka flavored with buffalo grass.

The three families waited for the first star to come out before eating. As they waited, they sang the old familiar carols by the light of the candle-lit tree.

Trina could not keep her mind on the food. She kept thinking about the packages under the tree. She had long since ceased to believe in the *Gwiazdor,* the bearded, fur-coated Starman who brought gifts on Christmas Eve. She knew where the presents had come from. The squarish, heavy package must be from Tosh. She could tell by its shape and weight that it contained books. Books! But what about the other package, the lumpy one? It would have to be from her mother . . . ? Trina couldn't imagine what it could possibly contain.

Finally the time came to open the packages. As the grown-ups relaxed with their vodka and ersatz coffee, Trina and Nina impatiently tore open their presents. Fabre's wonderful tome on insects! Mickiewicz's *Pan Tadeusz!* A collection of short stories! Trina could barely contain herself, and Tosh barely escaped strangling from the hug she gave him. Then she unwrapped the mysterious, oddly shaped package. A doll.

A *doll?* She turned it face up. Glass eyes winked

at her, opened and closed as she tilted the doll's body. Trina cradled the doll in the crook of her arm, but the doll felt strange there, as if she didn't belong. "What am I going to do with a *doll?*" Trina thought. "I'm not a *child* anymore!" But, seeing Ronka's expectant face, she hurried over and hugged her, too.

"It's a very pretty doll, *mamusia,*" she said. "Look, Nina, isn't she lovely?"

"Just beautiful," Nina agreed. "And just look at my ping-pong set!" The girls exchanged amused glances. *Mothers!* their looks seemed to say.

St. Stefan's Day dawned brisk and clear. Early in the day Trina and Nina told their mothers that they were going caroling, as children customarily did on December 26, and that they planned to spend the night at the other end of town because of the curfew. Roman, unsupervised since his mother's death, had no one to account to. (His father, when not busy building coffins, drank himself into insensibility.) Janek and Kasia made up their own excuses. The conspirators were now free to celebrate Christmas in their own way.

In their shed headquarters, they made final plans. They would split up on Zeromska Street, the three girls taking one route, the boys another. . . . They all looked strangely well-fed because of the paraphernalia concealed under their winter clothing.

The girls found the walking was easy as long as they followed the streets, but once they were past the city limits the going got rough. The roads were clogged with snow. There were occasional treacherous ice slicks. The girls were headed for a village some fifteen kilometers away. They walked and walked.

It was well past noon when the girls finally reached the small, birch-encircled cemetery that was the agreed-upon meeting place. They went through gates hanging askew on rusty hinges. Their destination was a musty, abandoned mausoleum right in the center of the property.

They made themselves at home inside the rusty tomb. Drawing bottles, rags, and matches from beneath their clothing, they set to work. Kasia soon arrived and pitched in. The boys, rubbing red, cold noses, followed. The conspirators worked silently, absorbed in what they were doing. They stopped only once to wolf down bread, cold fish, a few apples. Then it was time.

The siding they sought lay just to the west of the cemetery. They walked single file, trying to keep to patches of ground blown clear of snow by the wind. They didn't want to leave any tracks.

The sun was setting when they arrived at their destination. It was growing progressively colder.

They made a hollow in a haystack facing the direction from which the train would come, and crawled inside. They knew the wait would not be long, but time seemed to have come to a standstill. After what seemed like hours the sound of a distant whistle broke the silence. This was it!

Roman and Janek bolted out of the haystack, heavy iron bars in hand. The girls could not see much in the darkness, but they knew the boys were waiting for the train to get much nearer. The girls moved out from the haystack and carefully arranged their supply of bombs behind some snowdrifts. The rumble grew closer; the train approached through the night like an eyeless monster. The girls waited for a signal from Janek. Even in the black of night they knew exactly what the boys must be doing. They had rehearsed every detail again and again.

Suddenly the rumble became the screech of rending metal—the train had jumped the track. Shouts and the sound of boxcar doors slamming rang through the night.

"Now!" shouted Janek.

Trina struck a match and held it to the rag wick protruding from the neck of a nearby bottle. Kasia and Nina did likewise. Then the girls hurled their homemade bombs toward the source of the noise. Sparks arced through the darkness and flowered into sheets of flame. Suddenly night turned to day.

A blazing figure tumbled out of a boxcar. The

shouts took on a different tone. Machine guns began chattering. Again and again the three girls rose to their feet to throw their bombs, and then dropped back behind snowdrifts. Before long they heard a new sound.

"Planes!" Trina cried. "We've given the Ruskis a target!"

It was time to go. They had accomplished what they'd set out to do—this was one train that would not reach its destination. But where was Roman? Trina searched frantically through the snowdrifts.

"Janek, where's Roman?" she asked breathlessly. "Where is he?"

"We've got to get out of here," Kasia gasped. "Where is he?"

At last they found the carpenter's son, crumpled in the snow. They looked at each other helplessly in the reddish light. Roman was too heavy to carry. They would have to leave him beside the railroad tracks.

Janek emptied Roman's pockets and tied up the contents in a bloodstained handkerchief. Then he took a scapular from around the boy's neck. He tied everything in a bloodstained handkerchief and handed the little bundle to Trina. "Take care of these," he said. She silently stuffed the package into her pocket.

"Let's split up again," Janek said. "It's safer."

Trina and Nina walked away through fields lit by the blazing train. The whine of the swooping planes marked with red stars was like music.

It began to snow. Already the girls' tracks were being obliterated. They stumbled along like sleep-walkers. It grew quieter and quieter, until all they could hear was the faint *squeak, squeak* of the snow under their feet. The darkness gave way to grayness. Shortly they would reach home. Trina linked her fingers through Nina's and kept walking.

12

Trina sat on her bed, her back braced against the window. The book she had been reading lay face down in her lap, but her mind was still following the story. She was marching through the jungle, stalking the rogue elephant. . . .

"Trina! Trina!" she could barely hear her mother's voice as she marched down the jungle trail behind the native bearers. . . .

"I really don't know what's wrong with that child," Ronka complained to Tosh. "Either she vanishes for hours on end, or else she buries her nose in a book. Sometimes I can't get through to her at all." Raising her voice, she cried, "Trina! Trina!"

"Oh, Ronka, leave her alone," Tosh snapped. "Whatever you want her to do can wait."

"But—"

"But *nothing*. Leave her alone!"

Trina's world had split in two. There was the world outside, the world she shared with Nina, and Janek, and Kasia, and Roman—no, not Roman; not anymore. It was a secret world, shared by no one else. "That's not quite true," she reminded herself. Tosh knew . . . but Tosh was different from other adults.

Then there was the world inside. She looked over at the Christmas doll, which was sitting forlornly on the windowsill, and her mouth twisted in a half smile. Dolls! She picked up her book. Sometimes she felt that the inner world she held between her hands—the world of books—was the real one.

The day after the train wreck, Trina went to Tosh. "Want to go for a walk?"

They headed slowly toward the church square. It was empty except for some crows vainly searching the snow for crumbs. They sat down on a bench under the bare chestnut trees. Trina scuffed her shoe tips together and swept snow off the bench. Tosh sat and waited. He saw Trina's lips quiver for just a fraction of a second as she bowed her head and dug fiercely in her pocket.

"Here. These were Roman's," she said. She laid Roman's belongings in Tosh's hand. Janek had told her to take care of them, and she was keeping her promise. She kept her eyes down, trying not to cry. Tosh closed his fingers over the small bloodstained bundle and said nothing. They sat side by side, watching the birds, not touching, but very close.

"Someday soon I'm going to ask you to do something," Tosh said as they were walking home. "Will you agree to do it and not ask me why?"

He saw Trina's head bob—yes.

It was a gold and blue March day. Snow gleamed underfoot, crows cawed, and chickadees flirted through the air. This was a proud morning for Trina. She was now a full-fledged runner for the underground, and today, for the first time, she was being trusted to do a job by herself. She was to deliver a message. The night before she had carefully memorized a seemingly endless litany of words and had watched the scrap of paper they had been written on go up in flames. Then, just as carefully, she had memorized the word *"Ogórek"* and a set of directions.

By nine in the morning she was well on her way. It would have been hard to imagine a more unprepossessing guerrilla. Matchstick-legged, lank-braided, and pale, Trina was muffled in a conglomeration of old sweaters. Long, bandage-like strips of cloth were wound about her legs and over all she wore a man's baggy suit coat. She looked like a street urchin straight out of Dickens.

Her first hour's journey took her well past the outskirts of town and into the woods. In the summertime the forest would be crowded with mushroom pickers and herb hunters, but right now, at winter's end, only the trees were there, etched against the sky. Nothing but the faint squeak of the snow beneath Trina's feet broke the silence. She felt happy, important, and secure in the knowledge that a whole heel of bread was tucked into her coat pocket.

As Trina hurried along through the woods she became aware of a hum in the distance. Gradually the sound intensified into a roar. A shiny machine rushed past, kicking up fountains of snow. The hum receded, then grew to a roar again as the motorcycle spun about and came snorting back. It came to a stop mere centimeters from Trina's toes.

Seated on the cycle was a poker-stiff figure clad in the dreaded *Waffen* SS uniform. The man's eyes glittered ominously in his skull-like face.

"*Was ist das? Eine kleine Polische Bettler?* What have we here? A little Polish beggar?" he hissed, in a voice all the more menacing for its softness.

Trina stood, unable to move, staring into the officer's shadowy eyes as a bird stares at a snake. Slowly, the figure lifted a gloved hand and pointed.

"*Raus! Raus! Mach snell!* Out of the way! Move!" But Trina stood there hypnotized.

Suddenly the SS man was galvanized into action.

In one movement he was off the cycle; in a single stride he stood toe to toe with Trina. Sunlight glinted on the shining object he held in his hand as it arced through the air and descended on Trina's head. Over and over and over again he struck her. . . .

There was a voice in her head, Ronka's remembered voice, repeating: "Don't you *ever* let a *Szwab* see you cry! *Never, never, never,* NEVER let them see you afraid! Never, never, never, never . . ."

Then another voice took over where the first had left off—Tosh's voice: "Survive." Tosh whispered, "You must above all survive. As long as you are alive and breathing there is hope. Survive!"

And overlaying these voices was the harsh sound of the guttural German: "*Verdammte dreck! Sheise! Das kleine bettler!* . . . Damned brat! Little beggar!"

And silence.

When Trina opened her eyes there was silence again, and blue shadows lay across the snow. There were also red stains on the snow where her face had been resting. A thought flashed through her mind: the message! She was late. Very late.

She got up, and fell, and got up again. She had to get back to the footpath. "Just concentrate on one step at a time," she told herself. She fell again . . . and got up . . . and fell . . . and wondered why the pink haze surrounding her wouldn't go away. She wiped her eyes with a corner of her coat. The cloth came away sticky.

Then suddenly it was dark. The moon rode the skies, and there was a fire, and hot soup. A bundled-up man with a Sten slung across his chest cleaned her wounds with gentle hands. Other men with guns stood nearby. Somebody said *"Ogórek,"* and Trina struggled to sit up.

"Sleep, little one, sleep," a voice whispered, but Trina would not close her eyes until she had recited her list. Letter perfect.

Trina didn't forget the SS man. Six months later, when she had earned her own gun, she killed him.

13

Spring came in slowly, but finally the snow melted and buds swelled on the trees. The chickens moved out of doors, leaving their dusty, dimly lit shed to the four remaining Gray Knights. The conspirators hadn't done much together since Roman's death. Things weren't the same without him.

Janek mostly roamed on his own, and when the group met he said very little about what he had done. Trina and Nina saw him about the streets, appearing and disappearing like a ghost. They heard rumors of daring acts, but Janek never confirmed them. In contrast, Kasia stayed close to her grandmother's apartment, seldom venturing out. Trina and Nina came to believe that it was up to them to continue what the Gray Knights had begun.

They tracked down Irma Muller and began to follow her. After shadowing her for days, they concluded that she never went anywhere alone. At the *Kommissariat,* where she worked, she was surrounded by brownshirts. At night she went home with an assortment of officers who stayed and stayed. . . . But the girls didn't give up. They continued to follow her. And they found out that on Sundays Irma Muller could be found in her apartment alone. Good. Now they could begin to plan.

Trina's sense of planning and Nina's resourcefulness combined to make the girls a formidable team. They had become so close that, often, each knew what the other was thinking even though they hadn't exchanged a word. Without quite knowing how, they came to decide that Easter would be the day—or even better *Śmigus,* the day after Easter when she would surely be inside alone. The water spraying that was a traditional part of the holiday—a custom left over from pagan fertility rites—would provide the opportunity the girls were looking for. On *Śmigus* boys and young men roamed the streets armed with bottles, jars, and buckets of water, ready to douse any female foolhardy enough to venture out. Courtly swains sprayed their favorite damsels with cologne. Unwary farm girls got dunked in horse troughs and wells. Few females went outside on *Śmigus.*

Two weeks before Easter, Trina and Nina sat on the roof of the shed, concealed by the drooping flower-laden branches of the old pear tree.

"Where are we going to get the ether?" asked Trina.

"How about that chemist, Zymski, who lives at your place . . . think we could . . . ?"

"Perfect," answered Trina. "I should have thought of that."

During the week before Easter the girls haunted Trina's house. Ronka complained that they were constantly underfoot, but secretly she was pleased to see the girls so occupied with their dolls and homemade doll furniture. Tosh watched them with a puzzled frown, sure something was up, but said nothing. Secretly, he worried. Trina felt her father's watchful eyes, but remained silent in turn.

Finally, just as the girls were despairing of ever being alone in the house, the awaited moment came. Tosh was in court, Ronka had gone off to do some black-market trading, and *Pan* Zymski, who seldom left his room, was out. Trina locked the door on the inside. If anyone came home early she could claim to have done so for safety.

The girls began ransacking Zymski's room. None of his supplies met their needs. But suddenly Trina held up a liter bottle triumphantly. "Ether!" she whispered.

"Ether!" Nina echoed.

Nina produced a perfume flacon with a rubber spray bulb.

"Where did you get that?" Trina asked, still whispering, even though they were alone.

"Stole it in the marketplace."

Holding their breath, they unscrewed the top of the flacon and removed the cork from the ether bottle. Carefully, without spilling a drop, they filled the flacon to the brim; then they screwed on its top and recorked Zymski's bottle. Nina brought out a piece of well-chewed candle wax and wrapped it around the spray nozzle. The girls then concealed the flacon under Trina's mattress and restored Zymski's room to order.

When Ronka came back bearing the fruits of her expedition, the girls were sitting on Trina's bed dressing their dolls.

The next few days were fever-pitched. Trina removed Hoffman's dagger from its hiding place and honed the blade. Easter Sunday went by with the blessing of baskets, of bread and salt and *pisanki* (Easter eggs). And then it was *Śmigus-Dingus*.

Trina and Nina left their *podwórko* early in the morning, right after the curfew lifted. They ran through crowds of boys, getting drenched, and finally arrived at Kalinska Street. The house where Irma Muller lived had only one apartment per floor. They looked around carefully for Germans while boys and girls darted about them. Noise . . . confusion . . . shrieks . . .

The girls ducked into the entrance and rushed up the stairs. At the next-to-the-last landing they stopped, gasping for breath. After taking deep gulps of air, they walked up to Irma's door. When Trina raised her hand to the doorbell, she found that her knees were shaking. She pressed the buzzer. Silence. She pressed it again. From deep within the apartment came a voice and the slapping sound of slippers.

The door swung open and a tousled blonde head poked out. *"Śmigus-Dingus!"* the girls chorused. Nina raised the flacon and aimed a spray at the surprised face. The woman started to smile. *"Was ist . . . ?"* she began—but the question was never finished. The blue eyes blinked, closed, blinked. Irma slumped to the floor half in and half out of the apartment.

Trina rushed through the doorway and encircled the woman's legs. "Hurry," she whispered, "hurry. Let's get her inside."

Nina stepped around the blonde head and grasped a sturdy arm. The woman moaned, and Nina stopped long enough to apply another squirt from the flacon. The girls pushed and pulled until they could close the door. Trina slipped the latch, and turned to see Nina pressing an ether-soaked handkerchief to Irma

102

Muller's nose. "Nina, we'll want her to wake up," she said. "Don't use too much."

They stripped the sheets from the bed, stopping for a minute to admire their softness. Almost reluctantly they tore the fine linen into strips. Soon Irma lay on the floor trussed up like a Christmas goose. The girls sat back to wait until she regained consciousness.

The doorknob rattled. "Irma! *Liebchen?*"

The girls froze. Then Nina ever so carefully applied another dose to Irma's nose. They couldn't have her waking up now! They huddled together, waiting. The doorknob rattled again. The door shook.

"Liebchen! Liebchen!"

Silence . . . then the sound of retreating footsteps. The girls crept to the window. As they watched from behind the curtains a man came out from under the overhang, stopped on the sidewalk, and stared straight up at the window. Trina and Nina held their breath. At last the uniformed figure turned and marched off down the street.

Irma snored.

"Let's get this over with," Trina whispered. "Let's not wait."

"You sure?"

"I'm sure," said Trina. "Let's finish up and get out of here!" She pulled the dagger from beneath her clothes. Her knees shook again as she straddled the inert body.

"This is for Roman," she said, as she plunged the blade into Irma Muller.

"This is for Roman," Nina echoed.

On legs that still felt rubbery Trina walked to the desk and picked up a piece of stationery and a pencil. She sat down and began to print. When she had signed the note "The Gray Knights," she stood up.

"I'm ready," she said. "Let's get out of here."

"All right," Nina said, "but let's take this with us." She held out a neatly folded woman's uniform.

Trina nodded. "Good idea. Is there anything else we can use?" Nina opened a closet and found a second uniform, a man's. They would take that, too. Then she reached for Irma's purse, and hesitated.

"Take the papers," Trina said firmly. "Somebody can use them."

They rolled the uniforms into small bundles and stuffed them under their clothes. Nina, always roly-poly, now looked fat. Trina tried to choke back a giggle. As she walked by Irma's hall mirror, she noticed that despite her own generous padding, she still looked like a scarecrow.

Outside, bands of boys still were pursuing fleeing, giggling girls. Shrieks of laughter and outrage reached to Irma's fourth-floor apartment.

They cracked open the door and peered out, listening, ready to jump back inside. The staircase was deserted. They slipped out and pulled the door closed. The lock clicked behind them. They hurried noiselessly down the stairs, stopped in the shadowy entranceway, then merged with a noisy band that was passing by. They ran along with the group, shrieking and shouting, getting drenched once again. Finally, hearts pounding, they dashed through their own *brama*.

Trina headed straight for her own doorway. She listened for sounds from within. Nothing—nobody was home. She motioned to Nina to follow her down to the *piwnica*. In the old wine cellar they pulled the uniforms from beneath their clothing. Trina found that her cubbyhole was too small to hold everything, so she rerolled one of the uniforms and hurried through the subterranean warren to Tosh's hiding place. She would stash the rest of the clothing there.

Trina rejoined Nina at the top of the dark stairs. Together they went outside and sat down on the stoop. Before long the sun had dried their wet clothes and warmed them.

14

During the rest of April and all through May, Trina and Nina made daily trips to the Church of St. Agnieszka for catechism lessons. They were getting ready for their first communion. In happy anticipation Ronka scoured the black market for material suitable for a communion dress. At last she found what she had been looking for: a length of white prewar silk. She bore it home with great pride. "Look, Tosh, isn't it beautiful?" she exclaimed. "And all it cost me was a side of bacon and three months' ration coupons!"

Further negotiations produced enough leather and white linen for a pair of white slippers. One of Nina's uncles agreed to make the slippers in exchange for another length of silk. Ronka also found, and bartered for, an enormous taffeta hair ribbon and a wreath of wax flowers.

With each acquisition Ronka grew more enthusiastic, but Trina viewed the preparations in near panic. The goings-on meant only one thing for her: CONFESSION! At the very thought of it her mouth became as dry as sawdust and her knees turned to water.

"I won't go," she thought. "I won't go. I won't." Then with a shiver, she whispered to herself, "But I have to!"

As the dreaded day grew nearer, Trina realized that Nina was as frightened of confession as she was. "Maybe we won't pass the test," she said hopefully to Trina one day in the poultry shed.

"But we know all the answers," Trina replied glumly.

"Do you think it's really true that priests can't repeat anything they hear in confession?"

"That's what Tosh says, so it must be so," Trina said firmly. But she still felt afraid, and so did her best friend.

"Who do you think we should go to?" Nina asked after a long silence. "Father Kaczmarski?"

"No. He's so old, and he looks so mean."

"Father Piwniarski?"

"I don't—" Trina began. Then she suddenly brightened. "I know—Father Pilczak. He's the one who always plays *berek* with the boys and kicks the ball. The one with the red face and bald head. The one who's always telling jokes . . ."

The fateful day arrived. Trina scrubbed her face until it gleamed, rubbed her ears vigorously with the gritty soap, braided her hair so tightly that her eyes were pulled back at the corners, and spit-shined her shoes. She was ready. Solemnly she crossed the *podwórko*. Instead of throwing stones at Nina's window, as usual, she entered the hallway, walked up a flight of stairs, and knocked on the door. Nina, looking unnaturally neat and clean, stood waiting inside her apartment.

The two girls set out for church, walking slowly. Other young people—singly, in pairs, and in groups—were drifting in the same direction. Trina and Nina stopped to look at every window display along the way, delaying their arrival at the church as long as possible.

The Church of St. Agnieszka was built of white stone and topped with innumerable little gilded domes. The largest of them had borne an immense bronze cross before the war—the Germans had confiscated it "for the glory of the *Führer.*" Inside, the church was a rococo explosion of twisted columns, plump angels, a blue star-spangled ceiling, convoluted carvings, portraits of saints, holy statues on carved pedestals, crimson walls, multicolored windows (each portraying a different scene), silver organ pipes . . . There wasn't a centimeter of space that was not ornately adorned in some way.

The girls entered the church through the central portals, dipped their knees toward the altar, and joined the line headed toward Father Pilczak's confessional. Every few minutes the line advanced toward the wooden cubicle hung with crimson velvet drapes.

At last the carved fretwork screen loomed before Trina. She took a final step forward, knelt on the riser, crossed herself, and plunged in. "Forgive me Father for I have sinned . . ." She rattled on, hurrying her words before her courage failed her. When she had finished, she was totally out of breath. For a while she heard nothing. Then the priest spoke in a voice so low and muffled she could barely hear the words. "Yes, Father," she answered. "Yes."

Trina got up, her hands still clasped together, and left the confessional. She slid into a pew and sat down, dazed. Was that all there was to it? She knelt, resting her arms on the back of the pew before her, and began saying her penance. Soon she felt Nina slide in beside her and kneel in turn. Trina glanced sideways and saw her friend's lips move in prayer.

"Phew!" Trina said as they walked out of the church. "I'm glad that's finally over with!"

"So am I!" Nina said emphatically. "Let's get out of here."

They skipped over the cracks in the sidewalk on the way home.

Sunday—the day of Trina's first communion. Everybody was up early. All night long Trina had struggled to sleep on the curlers Ronka had manufactured out of rolls of paper that felt as hard as wood. Now her hair hung in long sausage curls and was topped with a preposterously stiff taffeta bow. A wreath of wax orange blossoms encircled her head. A garter belt held her long white stockings in place. Trina had gaped at the strange contraption the night before. Was she really expected to wear such a thing? Her white slip felt cold and slippery against her body. The high collar of her ruffled dress nearly choked her. Her hands were encased in immaculate gloves. Trina felt that she would crack if she moved.

They were ready! Tosh had brushed his blue Sunday suit with acorn coffee to camouflage its shininess. Ronka wore a flower-sprigged dress, and her hair was waved for the occasion. At the last minute Trina picked up the porcelain rosary and the white-bound missal that she was to carry through the ceremonies. They trooped out the door and into the courtyard to meet Nina and her parents. They would all walk to church together.

Nina, too, was dressed in unfamiliar finery. Her corkscrew curls were a shorter version of Trina's— for the past few months Janina had refused to let

Nina cut her hair to its customary shortness. (Nina was determined that as soon as the fuss was over she would crop it off.) She, too, had a stiff bow perched on her head; she, too, was wearing a wreath of wax flowers.

The two families formed a little procession, the girls in front, the parents behind. The grown-ups chattered away, comparing what they had invested in their daughters' communion and talking about the party that was to follow. Though the girls exchanged amused glances, they never said a word.

As they neared the church they began to meet other groups headed the same way. The girls were all in white, the boys self-conscious in long pants and ties. In front of the church, parents and children separated. The parents walked inside and took seats; the children gathered in the sacristy. Priests bustled about giving last-minute instructions. Finally everyone was lined up. At the sound of the organ the children marched out of the sacristy and into the nave. The altar was banked with so many flowers that it was almost hidden from view. Smoke from the incense burners carried by the altar boys rose toward the ceiling. . . .

As the first pair of children stepped out of the sacristy, the entire congregation rose. The music became deafening as the congregation began to sing: "Ave, Ave, Ave, Mari-ee-aaaaaaaaaa . . ."

"What am I doing here?" Trina thought as she

stepped up to the rail. The haze from the incense burners and from dozens of candles, the overpowering aroma of carnations and lilies, the music—all combined to produce a dreamlike feeling. Trina felt as if she were moving under water . . . slowly . . . so slowly. . . .

Back outside the church, Trina gulped down air. She had felt perilously close to being ill throughout the service. "Home," she thought, "home and out of these ridiculous clothes." Tosh and Ronka were walking slowly, nodding to acquaintances, smiling, bowing, exchanging pleasantries. "When I grow up I'm *never* going to church," Trina said to herself. "Never! Nobody will be able to make me! Father Pilczak is *wrong*—it's *not* a sin! It's *not* murder! Germans aren't people! They're *Szwabs,* vermin, cockroaches! Tosh didn't think it was wrong! All that praying . . . for what? I don't feel guilty. *I don't! I don't!* And I won't stop. . . ."

Later there was the party, with coffee and presents. Trina enjoyed the gifts but it was all she could do to pay attention to the guests. She felt as if her face had frozen into a smile. "If only they'd go home," she thought, "so I could get out of these things and meet Nina."

The Gray Knights had plans to make.

15

The knock at the door was so timid that it seemed more of a mouse-scratching than a rap. Trina, sitting cross-legged on her bed with *Gulliver's Travels* on her knee, wasn't sure at first what she had heard. She lifted her head briefly and listened, then shrugged her shoulders and returned to her reading. The knock sounded again, faint but persistent. Trina put the book down on the bed, slid off the rustling mattress, and padded into the kitchen in her stocking feet.

As she reached the door, the knock came again. Trina cracked the door open a sliver. A stocky young man was standing in the hallway, his clothes covered with dust. He had a bush of wheat-colored hair, and his mustache was so thick that it covered his upper lip entirely. He was twisting a billed cap in his hands. Trina noticed a horsewhip tucked under his arm.

She opened the door wider. "What do you want?" she asked.

"Please, I'm looking for *Pan* Tosh?" he replied.

After hesitating briefly, Trina opened the door wider and motioned the young man in. She led him through the kitchen and *Pan* Zymski's room and into their own. She seated the visitor at their flimsy table, and then poured him a cup of the acorn-barley brew that passed for coffee.

"You'll have to wait," she said. "My father won't be home for a while yet."

"My horse . . ." the young man began.

"What's your horse's name?" asked Trina. "I'll take care of him."

"Tomek."

Trina slipped on her clogs and went out into the *podwórko*. After throwing a pebble at Nina's window, she turned to survey the horse and wagon that stood in the middle of the courtyard. She was soon joined by Nina.

"What's this?"

"A horse, stupid."

"I can see it's a horse," Nina snapped. "I mean, whose is it?"

"I don't know. I *do* know, but I don't know what his name is. He looks like a trashman." Trina giggled. "Come help me put Tomek in the shed."

114

"*Our* shed?" Nina gasped.

"Of course."

Trina grasped the reins, smacked her lips the way she had seen *droszka* drivers do, and tugged. "Come along, Tomek," she said.

The horse followed obediently. Together the girls led him through the *podwórko,* around the garbage bins, and into the shed. In no time the horse was unhitched and securely tied to a pole.

"Nina, go get a bucket of water."

The girls left Tomek and headed back toward their apartments.

"Where did you learn so much about horses?" Nina asked.

"From Stefan, when we lived in Warznica. Remember? I told you about the farm we stayed on."

Nina nodded.

Trina was perched on her bed again, absorbed in *Gulliver's Travels.* Every so often she would catch a word or two of the conversation between Tosh and the visitor. The *Andrzejki* had sent the young man to Tosh. The visitor was clearly in trouble— big trouble. German trouble. Tosh was coaching him in the answers to give at the trial.

Trina heard tales of war so routinely that she no longer paid much attention. This one seemed to involve some illegally slaughtered pigs that had been sold on the black market. As Tosh described the symptoms of a virulent pig disease, Trina smiled. The Germans were *so* afraid of disease.

The following morning, the young man was still there. His name was Maciek Krawicki, and he was a miller. His trial was to take place in a few days. Maciek was badly frightened. Unlawful pig slaughter was viewed as a form of sabotage, a crime for which people could disappear forever into the maw of the unknown.

By the time Maciek went to court, he had practically become a member of the household. Many had sought Tosh's help, but Maciek had come the farthest, all the way from Kilnica, a village deep in the woods beyond Warsaw. Warsaw! There was something magic about that name. Trina asked Maciek to tell her about the city, and was disappointed when he replied that he had never been there.

"It's a very long drive," he explained.

"But it's so close!" she cried out, unbelieving. "It's so close!"

Tosh and Maciek left for court in the morning not knowing whether Maciek would be returning. It was dark and Ronka was putting supper on the table when they both walked in, smiling. "It went very well!" Tosh announced. "They swallowed our story about the pigs being diseased. Maciek got off with a small fine."

Ronka and Trina heaved sighs of relief.

"This calls for a celebration," Tosh said. "It's been a real victory." A bottle of *żubrówka* appeared on the table. The glasses were passed around.

Ronka served up boiled potatoes and *żur,* a sour, rye-based soup—this had become their staple diet. Tosh poured more *żubrówka.* Trina finished her soup, then threw on her coat and went out to see Nina. They set out for the shed to take care of Tomek, moving through the darkness with an assurance born of familiarity. The horse snickered softly. After Trina had fed him a carrot, the girls returned home through the dark.

"Trina, I have good news," Tosh said when Trina got back. "You're going with Maciek to spend the summer in fresh air, out in the forest."

Trina looked at her father in utter disbelief. How could he do this to her? Banish her for the whole summer? Impossible! Then Tosh continued, "On the way to Kilnica you'll stop in Warsaw for a couple of days."

Trina opened her mouth to protest, but then realized what Tosh was saying. She would get to go to Warsaw. WARSAW!

"There's a doll I want you to deliver for me," Tosh said. He winked at Trina. "It's a nameday present for a little girl. Her father will be picking it up at our old friends' the Wronskis' apartment. They live in Warsaw now."

117

Finally Trina understood. She was being sent on a job. Of course she would go!

"There's one more thing," Tosh said. A greeting I need delivered. I'll have everything ready by tomorrow. You'll leave the day after."

Trina could barely sleep, she was so excited. All she could think of was Warsaw. At last she would see that great city. And she sensed that the job she'd been asked to do was an important one. Tosh hadn't said so, but she just *knew* it was important.

16

Trina lay buried in hay. Above the moving wagon white clouds drifted, obscured now and then by dense tree branches. Maciek sat on the wagon seat, dozing, the reins loose in his hands. Tomek, as if directed by some unseen driver, was heading north.

Shortly after leaving Radom, Maciek had turned off the paved road. Ever since, they had been following barely visible wheel tracks through fields and woods. They had started their journey early that morning, shortly after the curfew had lifted. Tosh had given Maciek some very specific instructions before seeing them off.

"You must arrive in Warsaw on Sunday morning. Not on Saturday, not on Monday. Sunday," he'd emphasized. And, turning to Trina, he had added,

"Repeat and memorize this address. It's where you'll stay until Wednesday. Memorize."

Trina repeated the numbers and the street name. She nodded. "I'll remember."

Packing had been simple. Trina owned only two dresses, the one she was wearing and another. The rest of her luggage consisted of a pair of shoes, a red sweater much mended at the elbows, a billed cap, and two pairs of socks, all rolled up in a large scarf lent her for the trip by Nina. She had tucked copies of *The Arabian Nights* and *Gulliver's Travels* into the bundle. Once she got to Kilnica, she would be glad to have something to read. She had also packed a thick notebook and several pencils. And, of course, the doll. Tosh had been very emphatic in his instructions about the doll.

"When you get to Professor Wronski's apartment, you must give this doll to *Pan* Stanislawski, *nobody else*. Do you understand? Nobody else."

Trina repeated after Tosh. "*Pan* Stanislawski. Nobody else."

Shortly before sundown that first day on the road, Maciek roused himself, stared at the sun, then at the tracks they had been following, and smacked the reins against Tomek's flanks. They began wending their way through the trees into deeper woods. In some places they could barely scrape through. Finally, after passing through a particularly dense thicket, they emerged in a small rounded clearing with a narrow brook gurgling through it. Maciek halted the wagon under a huge beech, jumped off the seat, and unhitched Tomek.

"We stay here tonight," he said. "Get down."

Trina crawled out of the hay and slid down from the wagon. Cat-like, she stretched her muscles. It was wonderful to be standing on the ground again. She ran to the brook and cupped her hands in the cold water.

"No, Trina," said Maciek, "over there!" He pointed with his whip. "Spring water! See how it goes in circles?"

Trina bent over the spring, watching the swirling water. Tiny fish no bigger than matchsticks, almost invisible but for the dark dots of their eyes, darted in and out of the current. Trina dipped her hands into the miniature whirlpool and gulped down the icy water. Then she settled on her haunches to watch the minuscule fish.

In the meantime, Maciek busily rummaged under the wagon seat. He pulled out a square basket with a lid fastened on by leather thongs. From the basket he drew a loaf of bread the size of a small wagon wheel with a dusting of flour across its top, and a hunk of white cheese speckled with seeds.

"It's dinnertime," he said to Trina. "Come eat."

Trina sat on the dampening grass, munching slowly. The woods around them were alive with sounds. There were hootings and tweetings and the *kumquat, kumquat* sound of bullfrogs. Bushes rustled, brushed by unseen creatures. Tiny eyes gleamed in the gathering dusk.

At last Trina climbed back into the wagon, rearranged the hay into a more satisfactory bed, snuggled down, and feel asleep. She woke sometime later to complete darkness. Voices whispered in the night. Trina raised her head carefully, trying not to rustle the hay. She strained to hear what was being said and who was talking. She caught a stray word or two: something about "Warsaw" and "important." Then sleep overcame her again. When she woke again, she couldn't be sure whether she'd really heard people talking, or had dreamed the whole thing.

Soon after sunrise they resumed their journey, traveling on through fields and woods. At noon, they crossed a river. Trina asked excitedly if it was the Vistula—the river that ran through Warsaw—but Maciek said, "No, not yet."

They camped again, this time between two enormous haystacks. Tomek promptly began chomping at the nearest one. Maciek produced a fork and pulled enough hay out of the side of one of the towering mounds to camouflage the wagon. Then he scooped out a smaller hole in the fragrant hay and said to Trina, "Crawl in there. We stay here tonight."

They were up again before dawn. Maciek repaired

the damage he had done to the haystack, and they started off.

Trina was beginning to get bored. There was nothing to see but trees and sky and fields. Maciek was carefully avoiding villages and towns, and Trina was starting to feel as if they were the only people on earth. Lulled by the monotonous sway of the wagon, she dozed and dozed. Her book lay neglected in the straw. . . .

She woke up to noise and confusion. This was it! Trina sat bolt upright, trying to see, hear, and smell everything. What she could remember of Poznań didn't compare to this! *Droszkas,* wagons, lovely parks—for Germans only. People . . . people everywhere.

Maciek was leading Tomek unerringly through a maze of streets. Hadn't he said that he'd never been to Warsaw? Trina wondered, but she was much too excited to dwell on the matter. At last they pulled into the courtyard of the largest apartment house Trina had ever seen. Maciek stopped the wagon, took stock of their surroundings, and pointed his whip at a door marked with a bronze number.

"We're here," he said. "This is the place."

Trina pressed the bell. There were stirrings inside, and then the door creaked open. Trina almost shouted for joy when she saw Professor Wronski's familiar face. But she remembered Tosh's instructions. "I've come to deliver a doll for *Pan* Stanislaw-ski," she said quietly. "It's a gift for his little girl. My friend Maciek brought me. He's leaving me here for awhile."

Maciek tipped his hat to the professor. "I'll be back at daybreak the day after tomorrow, Trina. Be sure to be ready. We have a long drive ahead."

The professor nodded to Maciek. "Thank you, young man." Then he turned to Trina.

"Come in, my child," he said. *Pan* Stanislawski has been waiting for you."

Trina entered the apartment as the professor indicated a man sitting on a leather chair underneath a window.

"*Pan* Stanislawski, there's someone here to see you," the professor said.

Trina walked up to the seated figure. The blonde, spare-figured man looked up from reading a sheaf of papers, his glasses catching the light. Trina felt vaguely disturbed; something about that thin, bespectacled face made her think she had seen it before. But that was impossible. Extending the doll, she recited the complicated message Tosh had made her memorize. The man took the doll, turned it over absently in his hands a few times, and then casually took off its head. He produced a pair of tweezers from his jacket pocket and proceeded to fish in the doll's body cavity. At last he extracted a tiny twist of paper. Trina watched the procedure with fascina-tion.

Finally the man looked up and nodded. "Good work," he said. His voice was cold and distant. "Good work."

Stanislawski left the apartment shortly after that, taking the doll with him. As soon as the door closed behind him, the apartment came alive. Janka burst out of an adjoining room. The professor's wife bustled in. After hugs all around, food appeared on the table. People popped in and out. It was a wonderful reunion, but Trina couldn't wait to get out and explore Warsaw.

"Tomorrow," Janka promised, "right after breakfast. I'll show you all of Warsaw. I promise!"

After the last guests left, Trina went to bed on the Wronskis' living room couch. But she couldn't sleep. Every time she dozed off, Stanislawski's face swam into view and she woke up with a start. Where had she seen him before?

She was standing in the square in front of the church. Before her the gaunt outlines of the gallows stood like a forest of nightmarish trees. A priest was raising a monstrance in a blessing—it melted and coalesced again into a headless doll. An SS man was reaching for the doll—an SS man with blonde hair and dark eyebrows that slowly changed color to match his hair. A red slash across his cheek wavered and paled. . . . Tosh's voice whispered, "Remember . . . remember."

Trina flung aside her bedclothes. "Professor!" she

shouted. "Professor!" She ran across the room, frantically searching for a doorway. Something crashed to the floor and splintered.

The professor appeared in the threshold, a kerosene lamp in his hand. "Trina, my pet, what is it? Did you have a nightmare?"

"Professor! Professor! You must stop him! That Stanislawski!"

The professor set the lamp on a table. He drew the trembling girl close and hugged her. "Now, now," he said soothingly. "What's all this about Stanislawski?"

"He's SS!" The words came tumbling out of Trina's mouth. "He's SS! I know it, Professor. I know it!"

"What you're saying is a very serious thing, Trina," said the professor gently. "Suppose you tell me how you know?"

"At the hanging in Radom. Last year. I saw! I saw him! In uniform. He tried to stop Father Zielinski from approaching the prisoners. Tosh told me never to forget that day. . . . I know! I know!"

The professor suddenly looked very old and weary. He sank heavily onto the edge of the couch as if he were undecided about what to do. Finally he raised his head. "Not much time. Janka! Maryla! We have things to do!"

"It has to be done before the curfew lifts, before daylight," the professor said urgently.

126

As Trina watched, bewildered and frightened, Janka vanished into her bedroom. Soon she emerged with a stack of carefully folded clothing and a pair of blindingly shiny boots. Meanwhile, the professor's wife hurried out of the apartment. She returned shortly with a young man in tow. The newcomer also carried a heap of folded clothes and a pair of shiny boots. He and the professor vanished into another room.

"Do I look convincing enough?" a voice asked minutes later. Trina looked up and then shrank back in her chair. In front of her, in the typical spraddle-legged pose, stood a German officer. Buttons shone in the lamplight, boots gleamed, even the leather gloves gave off a faint glimmer, as if they, too, had been polished to perfection. Behind the professor stood a young adjutant, equally spit-and-polish. Trina stared uncomprehendingly.

"We go to arrest a spy," the professor whispered. "A traitor to the *Führer*. Heil Hitler!" And the professor's arm shot out in the Nazi salute.

Church bells were ringing high noon when footsteps approached the apartment door. Three weary heads lifted and turned questioningly toward the sound. A key rasped in the lock. The door opened slowly. Two peasants walked in.

"We got there in time. It's finished. Over and done with," the professor said.

Trina picked up her book.

17

Trina could hardly breathe. She clutched Janka's hand. There was so much to see! It was overwhelming. The sights! The sounds! The smells! People . . . people everywhere! All rushing . . .

The open market—their first stop—was bewildering. So many stalls—never had she seen so many things. Rugs spilled over cobblestones; huge hunks of gory meat swung from hooks, surrounded by buzzing flies; baskets were heaped with mushrooms . . . books! Trina stopped, transfixed. Books! Hundreds of them, row after row lined up on a makeshift table. Her hand dove into the pocket of her skirt. She knew to the *grosz* how much money she had, but recounted it all the same. Enough! Just enough for one. Trina pushed into the shoppers and squirmed over to the table.

Arabian Nights. In Desert and Wilderness. Panta-deusz by Mickiewicz . . . Trina's head spun. Her eyes jumped from one fat spine to the next—she had automatically rejected the thin books. She was going to get the biggest book she could afford. *Quo Vadis?* Maybe . . . no . . . ummmm, no, not this one either. *Sirs and Aces?* She flipped through the pages. Back to *In Desert and Wilderness* . . .

"*Pani,* for this worn-out book—"

"You little ragbag! Not a *grosz* less than—"

"Look at this cracked binding! There's a page missing—"

"A page missing? A page missing! Such a perfectionist . . . a page missing!" And the red-faced peddler woman thrust her fist under Trina's nose. "I'll let you have this book for forty *zloty* and not a *grosz* less!"

Trina threw the book back onto the pile and turned her back. She began walking slowly away.

"Wait—thirty-five!" the peddler woman shouted.

Trina turned quickly. "I'll take it," she said.

Her new purchase tucked under her arm, Trina followed Janka happily as the older girl went about grocery shopping. Each purchase, like Trina's own, was preceded by haggling over the price.

Janka's string bag filled up slowly. Here she bought mushrooms, there a live duck destined to be used for *czarnina,* the sweet-sour blood soup. The duck, stuffed unceremoniously into the string bag, protested loudly until its quack became just a hoarse wheeze. Potatoes were piled over it. At one point Janka stopped, exasperated with the wildly gyrating parcel, and attempted to rearrange the load. With a great flapping of wings the dinner extricated itself from the meshes of the bag and waddled off at an incredible pace.

Janka and Trina gazed at each other for one stupefied moment and then rushed after their rapidly retreating soup. Trina slipped on the cobblestones, dodged shoppers, ducked between stalls and around piles of merchandise. Her feet hit a slimy cabbage leaf and flew out from under her, but she shouted in triumph—as she felt her fingers closed on an outstretched wing. The dinner was safe!

Back at the apartment, the professor's wife provided soap and warm water. Trina washed away the dirt and blood, and examined her torn stockings.

"Here, Trina, give those to me. I'll mend them," Maryla said.

Trina peeled off her stockings and then slipped back into her wooden-soled shoes. She was impatient to get back outside. She wanted to see as much as possible of Warsaw during her brief stay. "I'll be back before curfew," she said.

"Don't get lost," chorused Janka and Maryla.

"I won't. Don't worry. Save me some *czarnina.*" And Trina was out the door.

Trina wandered down one street and up another. Here an old church caught her eye, there a palace, forbidden to her and her countrymen now, but still there to be looked at through the fence.

She descended steeply staircased streets and picked her way over cobbles slippery with age. She strolled down the long Krakowskie Przedmiesle to the Plac Zamkowski, where old King Zygmunt surveyed his city from atop a tall column. There were kilometers of streets to explore. Here a statue of Mickiewicz stood; there Kopernik sat with the world cradled in stone hands. Trina walked on and on, drinking it all in. So much to see. So little time.

Trina was nearly breathless when she finally turned the corner of the professor's street. Deep shadows covered the pavement. Janka stood in the *brama.* "We were worried," she said.

"You shouldn't have been. I would never get lost," Trina replied.

Soon she was ensconced at the table before a steaming bowl of *czarnina.* Potato dumplings floated in the thick broth.

"Eat, eat," urged the professor's wife, handing Trina a plate. "We've saved the *łapki* for you."

There they were! Two duck feet with the giblets impaled upon them, wrapped like miniature mummies in bandages made out of the intestines. Trina sighed. This was pure bliss!

18

Maciek was at the professor's door early the next morning. Soon Warsaw was far behind. Day gave way to brilliant moonlight as Tomek plodded along, his hoofbeats muffled in the sandy road that wound its way through seemingly endless woods. There were hootings and rustlings in the trees; something moved along the road. Trina sat snuggled into the hay and listened to the small noises. Tomek seemed to know the way. He shied briefly as something skittered across the road, followed by a slinking shadow. Trina shivered. Was it a fox? In a moment the shadow was gone.

Moonlight glinted on a carved roadside shrine. They had reached a crossroads. Tomek turned to the left undirected. The wagon wheels squeaked faintly. Trina heard a barely audible humming sound somewhere ahead. Maciek straightened up in his seat. "We're almost home," he said. "Hear the water? That's the mill."

The sound grew louder. The wagon turned into a narrow road that widened into a clearing. A huge wheel attached to an irregularly shaped heap of a building loomed ahead. To the right stood a thatched barn, to the left a farmhouse. Maciek climbed off the wagon, handed Trina down, and began to unharness the horse.

Two wolf-like dogs emerged silently from the barn and circled around Trina, their cold noses touching her knees. She froze.

"Kokus! Zolka!" Maciek said sharply. The two dogs wheeled around and trotted back indoors.

While Maciek led Tomek to his stall, Trina waited, her bundle clutched in her hands. In a few moments Maciek reappeared.

"Come," he said. Together they entered the house.

An oil lamp burned weakly on the kitchen table, its flame doing little to illuminate the shadowy room. Maciek picked up the lantern and led Trina through a doorway. She found herself in a small room dominated by a bed the likes of which she had never seen before. It was so high off the ground that its striped coverlet nearly reached Trina's nose. Piles of pillows were heaped at the foot and head. Each pillow was edged with a wide lace flounce.

The room also held a stand with a crockery bowl and pitcher on it; an ornate mirror; and a curlicued bench.

Maciek stripped off the cascades of pillows layer by layer, and placed the pillows on the bench. After turning back the striped cover, he paused for a moment. "Wait, Trina," he said. He hurried out of the room and returned a minute later with a three-legged stool, which he placed at the bedside. "I'll leave the lamp here," he said. "Sleep well."

Trina stripped down to her underwear, and then stood on the stool and climbed into bed. The mattress rustled beneath her; the smell of fresh straw rose up through the sheets; a huge pillow threatened to envelop her head. "This must be a giant's bed," she thought just before falling asleep. "A giant's bed for sure."

Trina stared in amazement at the walls surrounding her. In the dim lamplight of the previous night she had not noticed the brilliant frieze of the *wycinanki* running in a continuous strip just below the ceiling. Additional brightly colored cutouts covered the uncurtained windowpanes. There were scarlet roosters, peacocks displaying their tails, flowers that surely had never grown anywhere but in the artist's imagination, wonderfully gnarled trees, mushrooms, and butterflies. Trina sat for a while in the middle of the huge bed, absorbed by the shapes and colors.

Then she peered over the edge of the bed, located the stool, and clambered down.

There was water in the crockery bowl. A cake of soap and a square of roughly woven linen lay next to the pitcher. Trina washed, then stood before the mirror and combed her hair, amused by the distorted, greenish image that looked back at her. She dressed and ventured into the kitchen.

The kitchen was empty. A round loaf of bread lay on the table along with a veritable saber of a knife, a bowl of raspberries, a jar of honey and a spoon, a pitcher of buttermilk, and a blue enameled mug. A scrawled note under the knife said simply "Breakfast." Trina sat down and pulled over the bowl of raspberries.

As she ate, Trina let her eyes roam around the kitchen. There was a stove with a sleeping ledge like the one in Stefan's house at Warznica, but here the floors were of wood scrubbed to the color of pale straw, rather than beaten dirt. The unvarnished furniture was intricately carved, with an ornate pattern burnt into the wood. The whole room was awash with color, for the sun filtered through the paper cutouts covering the windowpanes. The door stood wide open, and a huge gray speckled hen squatted on the sill. Three gray cats stared unblinkingly at Trina from the stove ledge.

As Trina moved toward the doorway the chicken gave a disgruntled squawk and moved off to squat on the steps. In the light of day, Trina could see that the enclave was surrounded on three sides by trees. On the fourth side stood the mill. The wheel was turning. Wagons stood in front of the thatched building—a half dozen perhaps. Chickens strutted about. The two wolf-like dogs were lounging in the shade; they lifted their heads briefly as Trina slowly crossed the yard. A sudden hiss made her turn just in time to see a vicious-looking gander bearing down upon her. Trina took to her heels, the bird in pursuit. The dogs roused themselves and joined in the chase. Chickens scattered. A young woman appeared in the doorway of the mill, brandishing a broom. *Whack!* went the broom. It caught the bird across its long swaying neck. *Whack!* and the gander waddled off, still hissing. *Whack!* and he gathered speed, finally disappearing into the barn.

Trina thought that her rescuer was the prettiest girl she had ever seen. Her long braids were so blond that they looked nearly white. Her eyes were bright blue, her cheeks round and pink. "You have to watch out for that one!" she warned Trina. "He caught me yesterday. See?" She held out a purple toe. "I'm Wanda, Maciek's sister," she added. "Come on in."

Trina followed Wanda into a white whirlwind. Wheels turned, stone disks screeched against each other, dust flew. Belts crisscrossed the room, disappearing through holes cut into the walls; flails rose and fell like disjointed arms. A persistent thumping sound filled the air.

136

Pale figures coated with white powder carried sacks about. As Trina stood gaping, she felt a touch on her shoulder. Wanda beckoned her to follow, and together they went outside. It was good to be in the fresh air again.

"When the sun's overhead, that means dinner," Wanda said. "Go play now, Trina. Don't get lost."

"Go play." . . . Trina smiled. How long had it been since she had heard those words? Keeping an eye out for the gander, she wandered through the yard and into a little garden. Lettuces and radishes stood in neat rows ringed by raspberry and currant bushes. Trina plucked a few berries and wandered on. She stopped briefly at the edge of a stream to watch the mill wheel turn, and then wandered upstream to a place where the water spread out into a quiet pool.

The sun was high in the sky when Trina returned to the house. Her skirt was filled with mushrooms of all shapes and sizes. She tipped her treasures out onto the kitchen table: bright yellow *kurki* with fluted curly edges, white *prawdziwki,* brown-capped *koźlaki,* slick-skinned *maślaki* with buttery undersides.

After dinner Trina sat on the doorsill, cleaning her finds. Some, like the *kurki,* she threw into a pot; others, like the *prawdziwki,* she strung on white thread. When she had assembled a long rope of caps and stems into a fragrant necklace, she knotted the ends of the thread together and hung the string on a nail protruding from under the eaves. She would take the dried mushrooms home with her.

Trina carried the brimming pot into the kitchen. "For tonight's supper," she said to Wanda.

"With sour cream." Wanda winked at Trina. "Tomorrow we'll go to the village," she added. "You'll like it."

19

Trina loved the dunes that bordered the village from the moment she saw them. The golden sand . . . the shaggy, berry-laden bushes . . . the view from up top. Nearly every day that summer she picked her way through the thorny berry bushes and, her feet sinking into the hot sand, climbed to the summit of the dunes. From here she could observe the village unseen—the neat rows of houses, the roadway shrine surrounded by a minuscule picket fence, the silent, shuttered schoolhouse. In the distance stood the mill.

Trina would sit for hours watching the comings and goings of the villagers. Soon she knew which girl met which boy behind which haystack, whose husband got drunk regularly, and who was the best, and the worst, housekeeper in the village. She spent whole days on her sandy perch, occasionally dipping into her precious books. (She had to ration herself if they were to last all summer.)

It wasn't until the middle of her third week in Kilnica that Trina noticed something strange. During the midday siesta period, flashes of light seemed to come from the heart of the forest. They were so brief that Trina doubted at first that she'd really seen them. The longer she watched this curious phenomenon, the more puzzled she became. What could these strange flashes be?

Finally she could not contain her curiosity any longer. One sunny noontime when the flashes appeared, Trina took bearings as best she could and set out for the thick of the forest. Her bare feet moved soundlessly over the moss-covered ground. Sunlight filtered through the branches overhead, making dappled patterns on the forest floor.

Suddenly, so unexpectedly that she nearly stumbled into him, Trina came upon a man. He was seated on a log, his broad back to her, a rifle across his knees, smoking a pipe. Heart pounding, Trina crept into the underbrush and flattened herself against the ground, grateful that her tanned skin and green dress would make her nearly invisible.

After what seemed like hours, Trina screwed up her courage and raised her head to look about. She noticed a small clearing nearby. In it, a dozen or so men sat quietly. The guns slung over their shoul-

140

ders and the grenades attached to their belts told her who they were—*Andrzejki.*

Suddenly one of the men stood up. Trina swallowed hard—had she been noticed? The guerrilla raised his hands to his mouth and cawed like a crow. From somewhere in the forest came an answering caw. The man cawed again. Several minutes passed, and then, to Trina's amazement, Wanda walked into the clearing. She carried bundles in both hands, and, as Trina watched, began unpacking them. Out came bread, round white cheeses, and long strings of sausages. The men clustered around Wanda and passed the food around. Trina took advantage of their preoccupation to wiggle out of her hiding place. Soon she was speeding back to the sand dunes, to think.

She knew that she would never tell anyone what she had just seen. Nor would she ever again think of Wanda as merely Maciek's sister.

That evening Trina followed Wanda about like a puppy, begging to help with the dinner, with the dishes, with anything. Trina couldn't do enough for her newly elected heroine.

From then on, Wanda had an unseen shadow. Wherever she went, Trina followed, watching, learning, remembering . . . Her books were temporarily discarded.

She would have so much to tell Nina, even though Wanda's name would never be mentioned. Now she knew how to make chemical explosives, how to build a booby trap for motorcycles, and so many other things!

The evenings were also busy times for Trina. Either she sat with Wanda on the doorstep, sorting the day's pick of mushrooms, or she watched the older girl embroider the clothes she would wear at her wedding. Wanda was to be married after the harvest festival, sometime in September. Trina was torn between wanting to stay for the festivities and longing to be back home.

"We'll all get dressed up," Wanda explained. "I'll be wearing this." She'd hold up the white, wide-sleeved blouse covered with flowers worked in multi-colored thread. "I'll have a wreath in my hair made of bachelor buttons, red poppies, and gold wheat. We'll ride in a buggy, my brother and I, and the others will come by wagon. When we come back from the church I'll sit on a beehive in the middle of the kitchen and the old women will cut my hair off and put a lace cap on my head. Then everybody will throw money at me and there will be dancing and eating and drinking. There will be fiddlers and an accordionist. We'll celebrate for three days, and then my husband and I will go to our house!" And Wanda would fall back to her needlework with a new vigor.

As the summer drew to a close, Trina began preparing for the long train ride home. When the letter from Tosh arrived, everything but her clothing was packed and ready. The book she had purchased in Warsaw had gone into the bundle first, followed by the strings of mushrooms, a few brightly colored feathers, some carefully dried flowers, an assortment of smooth pebbles gathered in the stream, and a bird's nest she had found abandoned in a hedge.

The day of her departure arrived. Trina tucked her few garments into the bundle and tied it up. A second, smaller bundle contained gifts to her parents from her hosts. There were dried cheeses and a slab of bacon, a long string of sausages, and dried apples—a veritable bonanza of edibles.

Maciek brought out the wagon, put Trina's luggage in, and climbed aboard. Trina threw her arms around Wanda's neck and hugged her tightly. She knew she probably would never be back. People just seemed to come and go in her life—no one was around for very long.

"I hope your wedding is wonderful, Wanda," she said. Then she got into the wagon and settled in the hay.

"Good-bye," Wanda called, waving. "Good-bye. May the Baby Jesus and Saint Anthony see you safely home!"

"Good-bye," echoed Trina. "Good-bye."

The wagon creaked and swayed over the familiar sandy road through the forest. But instead of proceeding toward Warsaw, they turned east and pulled up at a tiny train station. Maciek took down Trina's bundles and purchased a ticket.

"Now remember," he said, "you get off this train at Warsaw." He scratched his head. "Then you have to take another train, Trina. A big one that goes to Radom. You'll have to ask how to find it. Maybe you should go to the Wronskis and have them help you," he added anxiously.

"Don't worry, Maciek, I won't get lost," Trina said. "I always find my way. I'll get home just fine."

Trina wasn't really as self-confident as she sounded. This was the first time she had been so far away from home. But if Tosh thought she could make it home on her own, then she would. She'd simply have to.

Soon they heard a shrill whistle and a tiny, narrow-guage train emerged from the trees. It was full of country people heading for the city. Trina took a firm grip on her bundles and shoved her way aboard. Using her elbows to help her navigate through the crowd, she made her way to a window.

Maciek stood by the track, twisting his cap in his hands. Trina placed her bundles between her knees for safekeeping, raised the window, and shouted, "*Do widzenia* . . . until we meet again!"

"*Do widzenia!*" called Maciek, raising his cap.

The train hooted and moved off.

144

20

Trina sat on the floor, wedged between an enormous pair of legs encased in cotton stockings, and a pair of once-splendid red patent-leather boots. She held her bundles tightly on her lap. The air was thick with the smell of sausages, bacon, and ham on their way to the black market.

The passengers were in high spirits, laughing and bantering. Somewhere behind Trina a voice began singing:

> The train is crowded,
> The train is smelly,
> I'm dealing in sausage
> And strawb'ry jelly.
> The *Szwabs* they search,
> The *Szwabs* they grab . . .

Other voices joined in. The mocking song was sung to the tune of an old Christmas carol.

> At black market I'll sell
> Ham, sausage, 'n' eggs,
> And strawb'ry jell',
> And buy me some vodka . . .

Everyone in the car sang the words of the chorus. Suddenly Trina found a bottle of pale green liquid being waved under her nose. She took the bottle, wiped her hand across the neck, and took a long gulp. A burning sensation bored its way toward her toes, making her gag; someone laughed and thumped her on the back. A hand proffered a piece of smelly fish.

"Here, girlie, take a bite of herring."

The hand and the voice belonged to the owner of the red boots. Trina eyed the fish suspiciously but took a small bite. Miraculously the burning in her gullet stopped.

"Good, eh?" the same voice asked. Trina nodded and took another nibble. The bottle, having apparently made the rounds, was back under Trina's nose. This time she took a long pull of the fiery *żubrówka* and then bit into the salty fish.

The atmosphere grew stifling. Just when Trina thought she might faint, the whistle blew a long blast. There was a sudden commotion as people began getting up and collecting their possessions.

"Are we in Warsaw already?" Trina asked.

"No. But most of us get off here. They search luggage at the station," replied the red boots' owner.

The train slowed to a crawl. Trina watched, fascinated, as one by one her fellow passengers jumped to the ground and disappeared into the woods. Soon there were only a few old grannies left. Trina got up stiffly from the floor and sat on a wooden bench.

"How far to Warsaw?" she asked a hunched figure. "How soon will we be there?"

"Not far," an old woman replied. "Soon, child, soon."

Trina gathered her bundles and felt her pocket to make sure her ticket was still there. The train continued to chug along, emitting an occasional whistle. Soon buildings began to appear at the sides of the track.

"Warsaw?"

"Warsaw," replied the old woman who had answered Trina before. Then she cackled.

Trina looked up, startled. "She looks like a witch," she thought giddily. "Just like *baba* Jaga in the fairy tale." Trina giggled. "Old, old witch," she thought. And she giggled again.

Trina hesitated on the train platform, trying to get oriented. Where should she go now? Taking the path of least resistance, she allowed herself to be pulled along by the crowd. Suddenly the surge forward ceased. Craning her neck, Trina tried to see what was happening ahead.

Uniforms! One by one the passengers produced their identification papers and were searched. One, then two more were led aside. Arrested. Trina watched as the old woman who had answered her questions on the train passed safely through the checkpoint. Taking a deep breath, she made a split-second decision.

"Grandma . . . Grandma!" she shouted, dashing past the guards. "I thought I'd lost you, Grandma," she babbled.

A German moved toward her, then shrugged his shoulders and waved Trina on.

"So, you're my granddaughter, eh?" the old woman hissed. "Fancy that. Suddenly I have a granddaughter!" She laughed. "Just long enough to get you out of here, you understand? Then you disappear! Understand?"

Trina nodded vigorously.

The train to Radom was late. Nobody seemed to know when it would get to the station. Trina had been crouching beside her belongings on the concrete platform for hours. She was almost unbearably sleepy, but didn't dare fall asleep. She might miss her connection. In an attempt to ease her hunger, she poked into her bundle and brought out a piece of cheese. If only she had brought something to drink!

A *kvas* vendor passed by. Trina dug deeply into her pockets. Only one square of pink left: fifty *groszy*. Not enough for even one bottle. She got to her feet and peered uncertainly about. Then she squared her shoulders and went into the station's restaurant. She sat down at a table and surveyed the clientele. No, they wouldn't do. A waiter, perhaps? Taking a deep breath, she signaled to an elderly man in a shiny suit.

"*Panie kelnerze.* Trade you some mushrooms for a cup of tea?"

The waiter raised his eyebrows and walked toward Trina's table. She delved into her bundle. Pulling out a string of mushrooms, she dangled it before him.

"Brazen little peddler, aren't you?" the waiter said. But his voice was kind. "Wait here."

"A skinny thing like you needs more than tea." The waiter was back, bearing a tray. "Buttermilk, boiled potatoes, and *żur*. And put your mushrooms away. What they don't know won't hurt them." He nodded toward the back of the restaurant. "Eat," he said. "Eat."

Trina fairly dove into the bowl of soup. She *was* hungry. And thirsty. The pitcher of buttermilk was emptied in record time.

"The train to Radom," she said to the waiter. "Do you know when it will arrive?"

"Nobody knows. You'll just have to wait. Maybe this afternoon. Tonight. Tomorrow. Who knows?" The waiter shrugged. "It's all transports lately—all going that direction, anyway. Nothing's like it used to be. If your train isn't here by this evening, you come back here." He picked up the pitcher. "There's more where this came from."

Trina grinned at him and gathered up her things.

Trina settled back down on the concrete. Drawing her knees up under her chin, she watched the milling crowds for a while, but her head sank lower and lower, until her face was resting on her folded hands. The noise of the crowd faded to a murmur. Trina slept.

A change in the rhythm around her woke Trina. It had grown chilly while she slept, and it was nearly dark. The crowd had stopped milling about and stood lining the platform, looking expectantly into the distance. There was a far-off rumble. The train was coming!

Trina was virtually lifted off her feet and carried onto the train by the surging mass of people. She clung to her bundles, desperately trying to remain upright. With the help of her elbows she managed to worm her way deep into the carriage. As she passed an open compartment door she spied a vacant bench, and wiggled herself into a comfortable position.

150

The train began to move. People sat, stood, slumped. Through the open door of the compartment Trina could see that the corridor was jam-packed. It was stifling. The windows were covered with heavy blackout cloth; blue bulbs burned dimly in brackets alongside the windows. Trina could barely make out the faces of her fellow passengers in the ghostly light.

The lateness of the hour and the immensely long wait were taking their toll. Snores filled the train. Someone nearby was reciting a rosary in a monotone. Trina settled herself further into her seat and closed her eyes. Occasionally, a change in the rhythm of the wheels woke her up briefly.

Once the train came to a halt and the Gestapo moved through it, shining flashlights at sleeping faces, but not requesting papers or conducting searches. A collective sigh filled the train when the Germans finally got off and the train resumed its journey. Bottles were produced and passed around. Hunks of sausage and bread were brought out of hiding. Someone began singing the same song Trina had heard earlier on the little train. When the vodka got to Trina, she didn't hesitate. She took a long swallow and passed the bottle on; then she joined in the singing.

After a while someone removed the blackout curtains from the window. The sky was tinged with pink. "I'll be home soon," Trina thought. "Soon, soon."

As the train neared Radom a number of the passengers leapt off into the underbrush. By the time the train reached the station, it was only half full. Just like the little train to Warsaw, Trina thought sleepily.

Trina climbed down to the platform on legs that were stiff and numb. In spite of herself, she searched the crowd for a familiar face. How could anyone have come to meet her? There was no way to predict when a train would arrive.

She walked toward the gates, following closely on the heels of several women, as if she were part of their group. The guard checking papers barely glanced at her. Soon she was out of the station and hurrying toward home.

21

Trina squirmed impatiently in the straw. She was bursting with things to tell Nina, but her friend just wouldn't stop talking. She had bubbled nonstop all the way across the *podwórko* to the shed.

"We have a school now, Trina," she said. "At Irena's house. You don't know Irena—she's very skinny. . . . There's a new boy in the class, too, Staszek. He lives near Irena. And Janek and Kasia, of course."

"A few weeks after you left, my mother and your father came up with the idea," Nina continued. "They said with everything so disrupted we're growing up like barbarians. Someone told them about Irena's mother. She was a school principal before the war. Your father asked her for advice and that's

153

how we got our own schoolroom . . ."

Nina stopped for breath.

"What are you studying?" Trina asked before Nina could continue.

"Come tomorrow and see for yourself," Nina replied with a toss of her head. "We've been learning things out of school, too. From Staszek's father and Janek.

"What kind of things?" Trina broke in.

"Just things," Nina said airily. "Like how to make a firebomb out of a bottle. It's really quite simple. You fill the bottle with gasoline, slip in a little capsule—"

"I know all about it," Trina interrupted. "You add potassium chloride and sulphuric acid—and it's two capsules, not one. When you throw the bottle the glass breaks, and you've got yourself a firebomb."

"How do you know that?" Nina was obviously astonished.

"Oh, it's just something I picked up while I was away," Trina answered nonchalantly.

Trina settled herself at the schoolroom table and began inspecting the others. The tall, slender girl must be Irena. Trina mentally christened her the Stork; she was at least a head taller than Trina herself and had impossibly long skinny legs. The towheaded boy who had come in with Janek had to be Staszek. He had a shock of blonde hair that kept falling into his eyes.

A large oil lamp stood in the middle of the table. The wick was turned up high. Tosh got to his feet. He was holding a long stick. An apple dangled from one end, a large turnip from the other.

"Today, my dear students," he said, "we shall discuss the solar system. If I spin the apple so . . ."

Trina sighed. She already knew all about the planets. With a yawn, she began to doodle on the square of paper before her—curlicues and leaves and flowers . . .

When Irena's mother began reading out loud, Trina laid down her pencil. She had never heard poetry like that before. "Could I borrow the book?" she wondered. She would ask.

Trina sat propped up against a chicken roost. The early morning light trickled into the shed. Janek was talking. "These little glass things are ampules that vaccines come in. Our people get them from hospitals. You need two for each bottle. You fill one with sulphuric acid—and be careful, this acid burns. . . ."

Trina smiled to herself and thought back to Wanda and the *Andrzejki* in the forest. If her friends only knew . . .

"We need bottles badly," Janek continued. "Any kind will do—from *kvas,* from vodka—it doesn't matter. Store them in your basements. We've got to be prepared."

"Prepared for what?" asked Trina.

Janek didn't answer. Instead, he pulled a gun from an old potato sack. Trina set bolt upright. A Sten!

"Anybody know how to use this?" Janek asked.

Trina got up from her grave mound and walked slowly over to Janek. She took the gun out of his hands, opened the magazine, and sighted along the barrel. Then she turned and faced the others.

"This is the magazine," she said, holding up the gun. "Here's how you load it."

The gun passed from hand to hand. Trina didn't stop demonstrating until everyone knew how to handle it properly. "And remember, you don't have to aim exactly. Just point in the general direction and fire. Watch out for the kick, though. It can knock your teeth out."

As they were headed home over the stubbled fields, Nina stole sidelong glances at Trina. Trina hummed as she walked. From time to time she gave a little skip. It was good to be back home.

22

It was a dank, foggy day. Mist hugged the leaf-strewn ground. Trina and Staszek walked under the dripping trees along the narrow, winding cemetery path.

"Let's try that one," Staszek said, pointing to an ornate mausoleum decorated with pointed arches, miniature flying buttresses, and gargoyles. Trina shuddered, remembering the musty tomb by the rail-road tracks, a crumpled figure in the snow . . .

They ran toward the stone structure. "It's locked," Staszek said, rattling the solid wooden door.

"Here—" Trina handed him a rock. "Break the lock. It must be rusted out."

Staszek hammered at the handle. "It won't give. . . ."

Then suddenly the heavy portal swung wide and they both stumbled inside.

Trina gasped. "Just look at this place!" She knelt in the half-light, tracing barely visible letters with her fingers: K . . . A . . . Z . . . I. "This was a prince's grave, Stas! Look . . . 1734!"

"It's perfect!" Staszek exclaimed. "Let's go get the others. Whatever we do, I'm sure *he* won't mind. Look at the way he was dressed." He pointed at the armored stone figure reclining atop the sarcophagus. "He was a soldier."

Trina hurried back outside. She soon returned with Janek, Nina, and Irena in tow.

Janek carefully studied the heavy lid of the sarcophagus. "I think we can pry this open," he announced. "I'll need help, though. Stas? Nina? Irena?" He drew a pry bar from beneath his coat. "Trina, stand watch. Croak twice like a frog if you see or hear anything."

Trina kept watch for what seemed like an eternity. To pass the time, she smoked. She was about to stub out her fourth butt when she heard the barest whisper of sound behind her. She whirled around, a knife flashing in her hand. It was Staszek.

"Come see," he said.

Irena passed them in the doorway. "I'll take the watch now," she whispered.

Trina followed Staszek into the dark mausoleum and approached the group clustered around the sarcophagus. The lid had been shoved partially aside. It was balanced on a spike projecting from the wall.

Janek stood on tiptoe, peering over the edge.

"What's inside?" Trina asked.

"It's too dark to really see," answered Janek. "You're the only one small enough to fit through the opening—unless we slide the lid back some more."

Janek and Stas linked hands. Trina stepped onto the improvised stool and, clutching the edge of the sarcophagus, pulled herself up and over. She hung by her hands inside the tomb. Her feet could not find the bottom. "How deep is this thing?" she asked.

"Just let go. I don't think you'll drop far. Wait. We'll get a candle," replied Janek.

Trina released her grip. She landed with a thud, raising a cloud of dust.

"Give me the damned candle," she said. "It's dark as a tomb in here." She giggled. "Dark as a tomb."

Trina lit the candle they had thrown down to her. A trio of grinning skulls gaped at her. She gasped. Glittering objects were scattered among the bones.

"What's in there?" Nina's voice called down to her.

"Bones," she replied. "Bones and a buried treasure."

"Treasure?" Janek sounded incredulous.

"That's what I said. Treasure. Look!" Trina bent down and grasped a broad-bladed sword; its hilt flashed with gems. She waved the weapon over her head. "Look!" she repeated.

Trina bent down again and secured the candle in a corner relatively free of skeletal remains. From among the scattered bones she picked up a gold ring. Red glints shone from its central stone. Then she said, "Janek, what in the devil am I supposed to do now that I'm down here?"

"Pile all the bones in one corner, so we'll have as much storage space as possible," Janek replied.

"What about the treasure?" Trina asked, picking up another ring. Metal clanked against stone as she kicked at the contents of the sarcophagus. A breastplate skidded over the granite. Another sword lay in the dust next to a heap of silver buckles.

"Collect everything," Janek commanded. "It can buy things . . . bribe guards . . . get somebody off. Your father will know how to use it best."

Trina set to work. Soon all the bones were piled neatly in one corner of the enormous tomb.

Trina squatted, reached into her pocket, and brought out a cigarette. As she smoked, she gazed into the empty eye sockets of the three skulls lined up jaw to jaw.

"Hey, Trina, are you going to stay in there forever?" Janek shouted. "Come on out."

A rope slithered down. Trina handed up the swords one at a time. Then she filled her pockets with the rings and buckles, and tucked the breastplate into her skirt. She spit on her hands and grabbed the rope. Hands reached to her when she neared the top. "Well?" asked her companions. "Will it do?"

"It's perfect," she replied. "It will hold a whole arsenal."

23

Trina traced a circle in the frosty flower petals on the windowpane, and then blew. A clear spot appeared, and she blew again, enlarging it. When she put her face close to the glass she could see the swirling snow outside. Trina imagined that there were mysterious figures dancing in the white whirling mass. "The Ice Queen has come," she whispered, recalling a tale she had read. "The Ice Queen has come."

Behind her, the cast-iron stove glowed redly. A teakettle whistled somewhere. Trina stared through the little hole in the frost. The blinding snow had been coming down for hours and hours.

She picked up a book and idly flipped the pages. Then she turned back to the window. It was snowing harder than ever. With a shrug, Trina got off her bed, put on her sweater, and slipped into the tattered man's jacket that she used for a coat. After flinging a long scarf around her neck and jamming a woolen cap over her ears, she went outside.

The air was bitingly cold. Trina flipped up her collar, shoved her hands into her pockets, took a deep breath, and hurried across the *podwórko* to Nina's. White powder billowed around her knees. It was like walking through a thick sea of feathers. By the time she reached Nina's apartment her fingers were numb.

The two girls sat at the table drinking ersatz coffee. "Any news?" Trina asked.

"No. I think even the *Szwabs* are hibernating," Nina replied. "We'll just have to wait until it stops blowing. Can you believe it's almost Christmas?"

Trina shivered. "Remember last Christmas? Roman?"

They sipped their coffee in silence.

Trina stood behind the wooden portals of the *brama* gazing into the street. In the *brama,* it was quiet and still. Outside, the wind whistled eerily. A few figures passed by, hugging the walls of the buildings. The street was deserted. There were no *droszkas,* no passing wagons. The familiar ruts in the snow had been totally obliterated.

163

Suddenly a snow-covered figure stumbled into the courtyard, brushing itself vigorously. Trina didn't recognize Janek until he removed the scarf that had covered his nose and mouth.

"Come on in," she said. "Nobody's home. It's too bloody cold out here to talk."

The stove still glowed; the kettle hissed. Janek peeled off his wet outer clothing layer by layer. When he set his shoes in front of the stove, they began to steam.

Trina made chamomile tea. They sat on her bed warming their hands on the mugs.

"This is a perfect time," Janek said. "Nobody's out. Even the guards stay inside. After dark you can't see a thing."

"What if it stops snowing?"

"It won't," Janek insisted. "It'll snow for at least two more days. That's what the old ones say. What do you think? Shall we do it?"

"I don't know," answered Trina. "Who can we count on?"

"You and me and Nina."

"That's three," answered Trina. "I don't think it's enough."

"Well, then—Staszek. And Irena . . ." Janek ticked them off on his fingers. "That's five. Five should do it. Unless you want somebody else?"

"Kasia . . ." Trina hesitated. "I don't think we can count on her anymore. She hasn't said anything, but—"

"I know, she seems to have lost her nerve," replied Janek. "Ever since Roman . . ."

"It will be five of us, then," Trina said quickly. "I'll tell Nina. You talk to Staszek and Irena."

Janek reached for his shoes.

The candle flickered. The east wind seemed somehow to have penetrated the *piwnica* with its icy breath. The children worked swiftly, speaking only occasionally. Strips of cloth and long strands of wire lay about them. Janek and Trina patiently braided the cloth. Nina and Irena then tied the plaits into long ropes and saturated them with melted wax. Staszek was splicing wire with the help of cutters and pliers.

"Think we have enough?" Trina asked, pointing to their handiwork.

Janek contemplated the coiled wire and the waxy ropes. "It'll have to do," Janek replied.

They met in a nearby church vestibule at nightfall, to make final plans. It was dark except for a few feebly flickering votive candles.

"You'll be going over the wall," Janek told Irena. "You can do it by climbing the big tree. Watch out for glass and barbed wire on top. Got everything you need? Pliers? Cutters?"

Irena checked her pockets and the ropes coiled around her body, and then nodded.

"Staszek, you will help Irena. Place the fuses tight against the wall. Pass the bottles over the top. . . .

165

Nina, your job is to go up into the big pine. You'll be invisible from below even in daylight. If you see or hear *anything,* give the signal."

"What about you and Trina?" Irena asked.

"We'll take care of the two entranceways. Don't move until we give you the go-ahead."

Trina set off at Janek's heels. They circled the walled compound. At one of the entrances, Janek stopped. He handed one end of a length of wire to Trina and waved his hand at a tree. As she walked toward the spot he had pointed to, Janek began unrolling the coil of wire he held in his hands. Trina passed the wire tightly around the tree trunk and secured the loose end. Then she tugged on the wire to let Janek know that it was in place. She felt an answering tug. The wire stretched tautly across the road was invisible in the darkness.

Trina scurried back through the snow to the place where Janek was waiting. They hurried around the wall to the second entrance and repeated their actions.

Hand in hand, Janek and Trina ran to the tree where Staszek was crouching.

"Ready?" Janek whispered.

"Almost. As soon as Irena gets back." He adjusted the long rope. "Here she comes," he added.

Janek and Trina heard rather than saw Irena's descent. Just as she hit the ground, they heard a

166

faint whistle, twice repeated. Nina's signal. All clear.

Janek and Trina swiftly added more strips of braided cloth to the rope hanging over the wall. Then Staszek poured on the gasoline.

"Are you sure you got everything?" Janek asked Irena.

"All the cars, the cycles, and the three big trucks," Irena replied.

"Ready?"

"Ready."

A flame flickered between Janek's hands. It streaked up the rope. The conspirators ran toward the church. Suddenly Trina stopped. "Nina!" she cried.

"Come on." Janek yanked roughly on her arm. "Run!"

They peered cautiously from behind the great church doors. Suddenly there was a muffled *whup!* and a fountain of snow, illuminated from within, erupted in front of their eyes.

"It worked! It worked!" Janek exclaimed exultantly.

"Nina?" questioned Trina.

"We'll just have to wait and see," Janek said.

Pieces of metal rained down. Something fell right in front of Trina's toes with a thunk. She picked it up and found herself staring at a can. *"Schinken—* ham," said the label. She stuffed the can into her clothes.

Back in the *piwnica*, Janek and Trina shared a cigarette. Irena and Staszek were examining the unexpected "rainfall" they had collected. There were boxes of candy, fresh fruit, cigarettes and cans with unfamiliar labels. They broke open a box of chocolates and passed it around.

Irena displayed the cuts on her hands and examined her ruined shoes. "That damned wall," she said. "Look what it did to me."

"Don't worry," said Staszek. "I'll steal you another pair of shoes at the market. Better ones."

Trina shivered. Janek put his arm around her and lit another cigarette.

Time dragged by. The candle was almost burned out. "I think we'd better go home," Janek said.

"Wait for me," a voice cried.

"Nina!"

"Where were you?"

"What happened?"

"It was beautiful! Just beautiful!" Nina laughed delightedly. "Did you see how it rained tires and seats? And just look at all the loot we've collected. Here . . ." She began pulling candy bars, oranges, tins of meat, and cigarettes from her pockets. "Isn't it a shame the vodka bottles got busted? But to think that we blew up supply trucks! They must have been for the big shots! And all the staff cars—*kaput!*"

she continued. "There's a big fire in the headquarters and they can't put it out because the hydrants are frozen. Oh, it was beautiful!" she repeated.

"Where were you all this time?" Trina demanded.

"In the tree! Everything was all lit up! I couldn't come down. Besides, I wanted to see it all." Nina dug into the box of chocolates. "Your trap worked," she went on, turning to Janek and Trina. She chomped on a caramel. "Sliced a *Szwab's* head off as clean as a whistle, Zzzip!"

"Merry Christmas!" Janek said suddenly.

Cries of "Merry Christmas! Merry Christmas!" echoed through the *piwnica.*

169

24

The sun was a pale, late-winter yellow with no warmth in its feeble rays. Trina trudged through the slush, her toes numb in their ragged wrappings. Passing wagons threw up gobs of melting snow with every turn of their iron-banded wheels. Horses plodded wearily through the mush. Trina huddled deep in her jacket and tucked her hands further into her sleeves—the left hand in the crook of the right elbow, the right in the crook of the left elbow. She much preferred the biting cold of the midwinter months to this damp, between-seasons weather.

It was over a year since the Gray Knights had blown up the compound. In the months that followed, Trina had learned to tape packages in the hollow of her back and inside her thighs. She carried a knife now tucked into her sleeve and a straight razor in her boot. School was forgotten. Books lay unread. In Warsaw she stayed at the professor's. But never for more than a night. After that, it was back on the road.

She sighed. Seven kilometers more. But at least when she reached the open fields the snow would be firmer and easier to walk on. She drove her hands even deeper into her sleeves, hugging herself. Cold bundles bumped against her bony hips as she walked. "Offerings for the ancient knight," she thought. But he wouldn't get to keep them for long.

Staszek and Janek were already at work in the mausoleum. The stone lid of the tomb had been shoved aside and both boys were busy underground. Trina smelled oil and could hear the click of metal. She handed her bundles down to Janek. "Where is all this stuff going?" she asked.

"Warsaw," Janek replied.

Trina shuddered, remembering the stench of burning flesh that had drifted out from behind the charred Ghetto walls the previous spring.

"What's happening there?"

"Nothing, yet," he said.

"What's going to happen?" she persisted.

"Something big," Staszek chimed in. "But we don't know what."

"How big?" Trina asked.

"I tell you, we don't know," Janek answered. "The old ones won't tell us."

"That's right," added Staszek. "They think we're children and can't be trusted."

"Children?" Trina said with disgust. "How could they?"

When everything had been cleaned and packed they climbed out of the tomb and shoved the lid back into place.

"That's a good day's work," Janek announced. "As soon as we get the word, we'll start moving all this. . . ." He gestured toward the stone receptacle.

"How will we do it?" asked Trina.

"In teams. Two to a team. As soon as they tell us the details, I'll let you know." Janek began pulling on his gloves.

"What about Nina and Irena?" Trina asked.

"All of us," said Janek.

"In the meantime, I'll get us some traveling clothes," Staszek put in. "Especially shoes." He grinned. "Have you seen Irena's new shoes?"

"Yes," Trina said, envy creeping into her voice. "Where . . . ?"

"From the market. Want to come along with me and pick out a pair?"

"Damn right!" Trina cried. "Let's go!"

Trina dug her elbow into Staszek's side and pointed with her chin. "Those," she whispered, staring at a pair of shiny red patent-leather boots. "They're absolutely prewar!"

"No good," Staszek snapped.

"But they're beautiful!"

"No good," Staszek repeated. "Look how thin the soles are. Besides, they'd miss them right away. How about those brown ones at the end?"

"Oh, all right," Trina sighed. "The brown ones."

Spring and early summer passed in a blur of activity. Trains and wagons, and kilometers of roads measured by weary footsteps. Barns and haystacks and damp corners under bridges and culverts. Riding on the cowcatcher in front of the train's engine. Jumping onto and off of flatcars, eyes smarting from the cinders. Lying atop freight cars and ducking approaching tunnels. Stealing fruit out of orchards and digging potatoes out of fields.

One June afternoon Trina and Staszek lay sleeping on grain sacks in a freight car. A change in the rhythm of the wheels abruptly woke them.

"Why are we slowing down?" Trina asked sleepily.

Staszek knelt at the door. "I don't know, but I don't like it. We shouldn't be stopping here," he answered.

Trina knelt alongside him and peered out at fields golden with grain.

"Jump?" she inquired.

"Jump."

They rolled down the incline and lay in a ditch watching the train lose speed. Finally Trina sat up and began picking gravel out of one hand.

"You all right?" Staszek asked.

Trina nodded. "Just skinned it," she answered. "We walk?"

"We walk."

They cut across the fields, heading north. Wheat swished about them. Grain whiskers tickled their faces. They emerged onto a rutted road lined with gnarled trees. Ahead were the outlines of a village. They sat under a tree, trying to decide if they should head for the cluster of buildings or circle around it.

"Something's wrong," Trina finally said. "Look." She pointed ahead. "No smoke. And listen . . . it's quiet. No dogs."

They watched a while longer, then turned to each other and nodded. They would go in.

The village streets were totally deserted. Dust devils danced across the cobblestones. Tufts of grass poked through cracks in the pavement. Their footsteps echoed in the stillness. The doors to the houses gaped open. Windows were shattered. In the square, in front of a large building with a star-shaped window, lay a heap of unidentifiable objects blackened by smoke.

Trina and Staszek stopped at the open doorways and looked into the silent houses. Plates still sat on the tables, flanked by forks and spoons. Chairs were overturned. Rags molded in corners.

Trina walked into a house and examined a scroll set into the doorframe. Then she picked up a book and flipped it open. Strange characters filled the pages.

"The *Szwabs* must have come through here," Stas said.

"Yes," Trina said flatly. She tapped the book in her hand. "They were Jewish."

"The whole village?"

"I think so."

"Where do you suppose the bastards took them?"

Trina shrugged. She thought of Hanna and the baby; she remembered the crowded trucks pulling out of the Warsaw ghetto. Where indeed?

25

July was warm and perfectly cloudless, a succession of sun-filled days. Sometimes Trina recalled the mill, the sand dunes, the green of the forest trees. . . . What was Wanda doing now? Was she still meeting the partisans deep in the sun-dappled woods? It all seemed so far away, so very long ago.

Trina curled deep into the straw piled in the shed and watched a sliver of golden light travel across the wall. Dust particles danced in the sunbeam. . . . The others would be here soon. For the first time since winter they would all be together. Tosh would be coming, too. . . . It was so quiet here in the shed. She was so tired. If she could only stay awhile and just sleep . . .

"This will be your last trip," Tosh said quietly. Five faces were turned toward him attentively. "And remember, all of you, you must complete your deliveries and be out of Warsaw before the first of August. It's very important. You *must leave* before the first."

"We're *all* going this time?" Janek asked.

"Yes, just this once. But you're not to travel together. Nina, you go with Trina. Janek will team up with Irena. Stas, you'll be on your own. You're all to meet at the professor's. And remember, you must be out of Warsaw and well on your way home before the first. Coming back, try to stay together. Not in a group, but close enough so that you can keep tabs on each other."

They got up off the straw and headed for the door. Trina lingered behind. "Tosh, what's going to happen on the first?"

"An exercise in futility—a gesture of the first magnitude," Tosh muttered.

"I don't understand."

"Never mind, Trina. Someday you will," Tosh said, laying his hand on her shoulder. "Go now."

Their last mission was accomplished. They were on their way home. The first night out, they decided to set up camp on the banks of the Vistula, right outside of Warsaw. Tomorrow they would fan out and travel separately, as Tosh had instructed them to.

Trina was wading barefoot in the swirling river water. Back on the shore, Staszek was laying out a feast. From his capacious pockets he produced an array of sausages, hard white rolls, apples with shiny red skins, and a dripping pickle. Nina squatted nearby, arranging twigs and branches into a bonfire. Irena, up to her ankles in water, was scrubbing beets and potatoes. Janek was nowhere to be seen.

When Nina had the fire burning brightly, Irena slipped the vegetables into the hot coals. Then both girls joined Trina in the river. The sun was warm on their backs. They dipped their hands in the cool water and splashed it over their heads.

"Come on," Staszek's voice floated out to them. "Food's ready!"

The girls ran through the lapping waves, giggling and splashing. The aroma of cooked sausage was irresistible. They reached the sand and collapsed, still giggling, around the fire.

They napped on the warm sand. Janek's dinner, carefully wrapped in wet leaves, sat on a bed of faintly glowing embers. Occasionally one of them would open an eye, rise up briefly on an elbow, and scan the riverbank for signs of their missing friend.

Nina was the first to spot him. It was late in the afternoon and the sun was beginning to dip toward the horizon. Nina dug a toe into Staszek's ribs and threw a handful of sand at the other girls. "Wake up!" she said. "Janek is coming. He's got someone with him."

They were all awake in a flash. Who was the newcomer? Where had Janek found him? Why was he bringing him here?

When Janek reached the fire, he picked up his food and unwrapped it. After handing the stranger a hunk of sausage and a potato, he sat down to eat. Four pairs of eyes bored holes into him as he sat munching slowly. His companion—who looked a bit older than Janek, but, like him, was blonde and freckled—sat at Janek's side, quietly chewing his food. His eyes wandered over the group.

At last Janek broke the silence. "This is Jurek," he said. "He and his friends—they're like us. He knows about the first."

Everyone sat up straight. The first! At last!

"Powstanie," said Jurek.

Nina gasped. Trina half rose and then sank back on the sand. *"Powstanie!"* she whispered. "An uprising? Day after tomorrow?"

"Day after tomorrow," Jurek said. "You can join up with us, if you want."

Trina swallowed hard. She could feel the pulse in her temples. She turned to Nina. "I'm staying," she said.

"So am I," Nina chimed in immediately. "Staszek? Irena?"

"Why not?" responded Staszek. "I'll stick."

"Me, too," Irena said.

Jurek got to his feet. "Come on, then," he said. "Come and meet the others."

They clambered over a fence. Bricks lay in untidy piles. Red dust covered the ground. Two-wheeled carts sat askew on narrow rails. Weeds poked their heads up among the bricks. Sand was heaped about; clay hillocks rose behind the piles of sand. Trina blinked her eyes. Pictures of Egypt and the pyramids flashed through her mind. "What is this place?" she asked.

"Brickyard," Jurek answered. "Since nobody's building anything anymore, it's been abandoned." He whistled. Heads popped up from behind the brick piles, the sand heaps, the clay hillocks. Bright eyes stared at them. Jurek beckoned.

From her perch atop a stack of bricks, Trina watched Jurek and his friends.

"This is Olka," Jurek said, indicating a girl with long braids wound about her head like a coronet. "She's our best shot. And this," pointing to a short, tomboyish girl with cropped blonde hair, "is Litka. She's an orphan. That," nodding to a black-browed brunette, "is Maryla. Maryla's a gypsy. She can't go out on the streets—she's too dark-skinned, they'd pick her right up. So she lives here. This," Jurek laid his hand on the shoulder of a chubby redhead, "is my sister, Anka. That," pointing to a lanky, smiling boy, "is Kaziu, our demolition expert."

Jurek turned to the remaining member of the group, an ash-blonde boy, impeccably dressed in a suit and neatly polished shoes. The youth drew himself up and bowed politely. "This is Tadek. Tadek's parents have become *Volksdeutschen* (Nazi sympathizers)—" Trina's indrawn breath was clearly audible— "but you don't have to worry. Tadek is one of us. And very useful, too—he speaks German like a native-born *Szwab!*"

"Tomorrow we'll assemble everything we're going to need," Janek announced. "We'll all meet here in the afternoon. The day after that . . ." Janek didn't finish. He simply smiled.

Trina stood in the middle of the great square in front of the royal palace. Her skin tingled. There was an electric excitement in the morning air. People rushed about purposefully; everyone was smiling. The movement of the crowd was like a dance. Trina wanted to jump and sing. "Tomorrow . . . tomorrow . . . tomorrow . . ." The words beat through her mind like a refrain. "Tomorrow . . . tomorrow." But today there was work to be done. She took off down the street like a hare.

Trina turned in to the hallway where the professor's apartment was. She leaned against the wall to catch her breath, and then pressed the bell. "Tomorrow . . . tomorrow . . ." She could hear ringing inside. She pressed the button again. Another ring echoed within. Nobody home. She'd never thought of that. There was no time to lose. She pulled a pin out of her braids and bent down to the lock.

Minutes later there was a click. The door gave when Trina pushed it. She carefully shut it behind her, and then moved swiftly through the silent rooms. In the library she found a piece of paper and a pencil. She hurriedly scribbled a note, folded it in half, and addressed it to the professor. After a quick look about, she propped the message on a bookcase.

Trina swiftly dragged a small table over to the great tiled stove that filled one corner of the book-lined room. She carefully placed a chair on the table-top and clambered up. Then she reached over the ornamental edge of the stove, removed a tile, and plunged her arm into the hole. First she pulled out an oilcloth-covered package; then she removed several other objects. Finally she replaced the tile and returned both the chair and the table to their customary places.

Trina removed her jacket and dress, wound two belts around her body, and replaced her clothing. She then put the oilcloth-covered package inside the front of her dress and buttoned her suit jacket tightly.

Trina surveyed herself critically in the mirror, tugging at her clothing. When she was finally satisfied with her appearance, she left the apartment, carefully locking the door behind her.

Again the excitement struck Trina like a living thing. She walked swiftly, bouncing on the balls of her feet, angling in the direction of the abandoned brickyard. At a fork in the street she paused briefly and then turned left, toward the marketplace. She knew she wasn't as expert as Staszek, but perhaps she could pick up a few things. Food would be important. She walked faster.

Trina wandered among the stalls and around the piles of goods spread on the ground. "Nothing that will spoil quickly," she said to herself. "Dried fruit . . . sausage."

As she wended her way through the crowd, Trina tried to stay hidden behind other shoppers. Every so often her hand darted out, and as quickly disappeared from sight. Each item that she deposited in her jacket pocket slipped through a hole in the lining. As the inside of her jacket filled up, Trina began to look strangely rotund.

By the time Trina reached the end of the marketplace, she was moving with some difficulty. She rustled and clinked faintly as she walked.

They sat in the lengthening shadows, screened from view by the high fence and the piled-up bricks. Trina had removed the machine gun from its oilcloth wrappings and was clicking a magazine into the breech. Then she pulled the ammunition belts out from under her dress and strapped them across her chest. A pistol was tucked into her belt. Hoffman's dagger protruded from her boot. Staszek and the others were polishing Mauser rifles. Tadek was drawing a map in the red dust.

"This is where I live," he explained. "Right across the street from the *Kommissariat*. We can pick them off from the attic windows as they come and go. We can stay in my apartment tonight—"

"Your parents," interrupted Janek, "what if . . . ?"

"My parents are traitors," Tadek replied quietly. His face was blank. Trina shivered. "I'll take care of them," he added.

"Come one at a time about fifteen minutes apart," Tadek continued. "Start leaving here in about half an hour. If you take the route I've just shown you, you won't meet any patrols." He got to his feet and meticulously dusted off his knees. *"Z Bogiem,"* he said. "Go with God."

Trina shivered again.

26

Trina sat slumped against a wall. Behind her, blue swans swam in golden lakes, dipping their long necks into the rippling water. A garland of grape leaves ran along the ceiling. Chunks of plaster had been gouged out of the decorative frieze; the pastoral wallpaper was pockmarked and stained.

Trina's jaws moved rhythmically as she chewed a wad of paper in a vain attempt to appease a grumbling stomach. Nina slept beside her, her head resting in Trina's lap. Janek and Staszek dozed, propped against each other. Irena, a bloody cloth wound about her head, lay curled up in a corner. Maryla, the gypsy girl, sat with her head resting on her drawn-up knees. She snored faintly.

It was quiet except for the sound of sporadic shots

in the distance. Nothing moved in the street. The smell of burning filled the air. It was midday, but a pall of smoke hung over the city, obscuring the sun; these days, noontimes were nearly as dark as twilight. In contrast, the nights were bright, illuminated by an eerie glow. More than once, Trina had thought, "This must be what hell looks like. Sunless noons and light-struck midnights."

She shifted her weight slightly, causing Nina to stir. Trina murmured an assuring word and laid a hand on her friend's shoulder. "Sleep," she murmured, leaning back against the wall. If only she, too, could sleep, but she was too tired, too hungry, too thirsty. "We'll have to move again," she thought wearily. They moved nearly every day now, from one set of walls to another, through streets they no longer recognized—all the landmarks were gone— past faceless buildings, around craters and pits, over mountains of brick and stone. Soon this street, too, would be leveled. Even now, in the deceptive peace of the early afternoon, she could feel the faint shuddering of the dying city. They had run and run until there was no place left to go. Nothing remained but a maze of bricks, an uncharted sea of crumbling buildings haunted by swirling winds.

"That first day," Trina thought, "that first day of fighting . . ." How glorious it had been! The holiday spirit . . . the singing in the streets . . . the bright flags hanging from windows . . . the red and white ribbons pinned to chests . . . the camaraderie—strangers smiling at each other, kissing each other. She smiled wryly—that first flush of victory. How the *Szwabs* had run! The metallic beasts conquered by bare hands—how brightly they had burned! Jurek's chubby little sister running, bare legs flashing . . . sunlight reflecting from a bottle held high in her small hands . . . the glinting monster turning in its death throes . . . and the bright red hair under the Panzer's treads.

The excitement of that first morning—the dusty attic floorboards . . . the row of tiny windows in the narrow space between the attic floor and the line of the roof . . . the knotholes in the floorboards creasing her knees . . . Jurek and Janek crouched at the same window, saying, "Wait . . . wait . . . wait till they're all outside. *Now!*" Tadek's impassive face, his toneless voice announcing, "I took care of the traitors." Trina felt a chill down her spine even now, knowing that Tadek had meant his parents. Later, running down the stairs three steps at a time, Maryla stooping to pick up a bright scarf lying in an open doorway and tying it like a banner to the barrel of her gun.

Was it still August? Trina could no longer remember.

There had been a house . . . was it on Wolska Street? Or was it on Piotrowska? What did it matter? There had been a balcony with scarlet flowers surrounded by great heart-shaped leaves spilling out of painted wooden boxes. The leaves of the plants

187

had hung in a cascade over the railing. They had knelt behind the leaf curtain, she and Nina. The distinct *tromp, tromp, tromp* of marching boots had approached from around the corner. A sudden spill of sunshine from behind a cloud—the sidewalk below the balcony had flashed with light reflected from thousands of bits of mica embedded in the concrete. Irena had slithered out onto the balcony, crowding between Nina and Trina. "Here they come," she'd said, sighting along the barrel of her gun. . . .

Trina lay with her nose pressed against the splintery floorboards. She blinked at the blurred images before her and gasped as the room came into focus.

There was a gaping hole in the wall where the balcony doors had been. Dust was just beginning to settle. Trina rolled over, into a sitting position. She tried to stand up and found that she couldn't. Pain shot up her leg. Her left boot was split at the ankle. Blood was welling out of the slit in the leather. Swearing, Trina pulled off the boot. She winced at the sight of shredded skin and torn flesh.

"Sit still," Nina ordered, ripping strips from her ragged skirt. "I'll bandage it."

"Shouldn't we clean it first?" Trina asked, inspecting the wound with a kind of detached fascination.

"With what, spit?" Janek retorted sarcastically. "Hold still."

Despite herself, Trina cried out in pain as Nina pulled the bandage tight.

"It'll have to do," Nina said. "Stand up and see if you can walk on it. Wait, put your boot back on first."

Trina took a limping step, then another. "It's all right," she said. "It hurts, but I can stand it."

They gathered up their guns. Trina looked around at what remained of the room. "Guess we'd better get out of here. The others?"

"Floor below," Nina replied. She clutched Trina's arm. "Look!"

A pair of legs protruded from under a heap of rubble. They began throwing aside broken bricks, boards . . . the legs stirred. Irena, her face powdered by fallen plaster, sat up. Her hair was matted with blood.

"You all right?" they asked her simultaneously.

Irena stared at them, then slowly shook her head. Lifting her hands to her ears, she looked at her friends helplessly.

"What's the matter?" asked Trina.

Irena looked at them in bewilderment. Tears trickled down her cheeks.

"She can't hear us," Nina said slowly. "She's deaf."

Nina took off the scarf she always wore around her neck and wrapped it around Irena's head. Then the two girls pulled Irena to her feet. Nina motioned toward the doorway. Irena grasped their hands.

Falling firebrands. Walls of flame on both sides. They ran, gasping, through the inferno. Somebody fell. Trina heard Nina scream behind her. She turned to see her friend's hair ablaze. She beat at the flames. Staszek took Nina's arm. They ran, stumbled, ran.

Trina looked with horror at the crisped skin on Nina's neck. Nina sat slumped, rocking her body.

"It's not too bad," Trina said, "Just a little singe, that's all."

Nina moaned and extended her hand. Trina gazed with horror at the place where fingers had been.

Somebody was shaking her shoulder. Trina started awake. In the dim light she saw Janek's face close to her own. "Come on," he was saying. "I hear tank fire. We've got to keep moving."

Trina rubbed her eyes. "Where are we going? Another house?"

"No," replied Janek. "This time we're going under."

Trina shivered. "The sewers?"

"The sewers," confirmed Janek. "Warsaw's dead. The sewers are the only place left to go."

They emerged into the street. It looked like the surface of some forbidding volcanic planet. The air crackled. Bits of fire dropped like rain.

"Spread out." Janek ordered. "We've got to find a manhole. Anybody got any ammo left?"

"Half a clip," Nina said.

190

"Give it to Trina," ordered Janek. "She's got both her hands."

They found, at the next corner, that the street was buried in rubble.

"Come on," Janek urged. "There's got to be a manhole we can open somewhere."

"But we can't stay out here!" Staszek hissed. "We'll be picked off like pigeons!"

"Keep looking," Janek snapped. "It's our only—" He broke off, bent down, and scrabbled amongst the bricks. "Look here!" The others crowded about him.

A sudden rumbling sound alerted them to danger. "Run!" Trina shouted, pulling Irena behind her. "Run!" They rolled over a low wall and lay, panting, in the debris. A Panzer was crawling toward them. Suddenly it veered and they saw Maryla sprawled on the pavement, frantically trying to get to her feet.

The Panzer belched fire. A ball of flame rolled over the fallen girl. Trina covered her ears, trying to shut out the piercing screams. Through half-closed eyes she saw a figure outlined by the glare leaping over heaps of rubble. She half rose, and felt someone savagely yanking at her clothes.

"Down, you goddamned fool! There's nothing you can do," Janek hissed.

Trina fired. Again and again.

"Idiot! You're just wasting ammo—you can't kill that damned thing with a gun!" Janek shouted.

191

Trina slumped down and shut her eyes. Janek was right. It was totally futile. She felt tears burning her closed eyelids. "What's the use," she thought, "what the hell's the use?"

"All clear. Let's get the hell out of here," Janek whispered. He hurried over to the smear that had been Maryla—Maryla—picked up a knife, and shoved it under his belt. Then he moved on to where Staszek lay, and with a grunt threw the wounded boy over his shoulder.

By the time Janek got to the manhole, Trina, Nina, and Irena had succeeded in shoving the iron cover aside. "You go first," Janek said, touching Irena on the shoulder and pointing into the yawning black hole. She understood. A moment later she had been swallowed up by the pit. "Trina, Nina, lower Staszek down," Janek snapped, preparing to follow Irena. He, too, disappeared into the hole.

The girls knelt and tenderly picked up Staszek's limp form. Trina swallowed hard at the sight of his crushed legs. With Nina's help she maneuvered Staszek's body to the edge of the manhole.

"Lower away," Janek called. The girls handed Staszek down.

"All right, now it's your turn," Janek called after a moment. The black pit engulfed them.

192

27

Warsaw lay smoldering. Kilometer upon kilometer of rubble and ruin stretched into the distance. Kilometer upon kilometer of blackened brick, shattered stone, crumbling chimneys licked by sporadic flames; kilometer upon kilometer of empty streets that echoed the sounds of marching boots and the rumble of Panzers. The sun was a barely visible disk, obscured by the smoky haze. From the other side of the Vistula, to the east, the distant chatter of artillery announced that the Russian armies were readying for the next push westward. An occasional shell exploded in the ravaged streets.

Underground, Trina listened wearily for the approach of the patrols combing the area. "Only a month ago," she thought, "only a month ago we were so full of hope, ready to storm the barricades with our bare hands. And look at us now. We have nothing—no hope, no ammunition, no food, no water except for the moisture on the sewer walls. All we've got left are empty guns, dead hopes, and wounds. . . ."

"Five of us," she whispered. "We're back to five again."

Janek—the oldest. The leader of the Gray Knights, from the very beginning. His face slashed by a long scarlet scar running from the corner of his left eye down and across the lips.

Nina—her best friend. Nina with the short cropped hair so like a boy's. Twelve years old. No fingers on her right hand; oozing burns on neck and back.

Irena—so tall Trina thought of her as the Stork. Turned twelve the day after the fighting began. Deaf. Head wounds.

Staszek—nicknamed the Fox because of his ability to steal. Blonde like Janek. Thirteen. Legs mangled by Panzer's treads.

"And me," Trina thought. "Skinny as ever. Also twelve. One shattered ankle. . . . Sewer rats. That's what we are," she reflected. "And we have the sewers all to ourselves, because the four-legged rats fled long ago. Had there been any left we'd have devoured them." Her thoughts turned back to the day they had gotten lucky and caught a stray dog. They had skinned the poor starving creature and picked the meat off the bones to the last shred. Raw. They had eaten it raw.

"Janek?" Trina whispered.

"Yes?" he whispered back.

"What are we going to do?"

"I don't know."

"We'll die if we stay here. How long has it been since we came down?"

"Days," Janek whispered. "I don't know—can't tell if it's night or day. A week—ten days . . . I don't know. I've lost count."

"We'll die if we stay," Trina repeated passionately. "We'll sit and wait and starve to death." Trina drew a deep breath and continued, "I don't want to die in a sewer. We've got to make a decision. I think we should at least try to make it out."

"I—" But before Janek had a chance to say anything more, Nina broke in.

"She's right. I don't want to die here, either. I'm for going, too."

"All right. We'll go," agreed Janek. "Now, listen. We'll follow the sewers as far as we can—north as far as Mokotow. From there northeast toward Piekelko. There we'll split up. Each of us will try to make it alone, or maybe in pairs. We'll decide that part later."

There were answering nods, more sensed than

seen. Then Staszek spoke. "I'll never make it. I can't walk, and I'm too heavy to carry. Janek?"

"All right," Janek said softly. "Trina?"

"I'll walk somehow," Trina replied grimly. "But I've got to find some way to keep my ankle stiff— a splint, or something."

"I have boots. They're good boots. You—"

"No!"

"Staszek's right, Trina. He can't use those boots anymore. Take them!"

"But . . ."

"No buts. You've got to. Now—let's sort through our things. We'll have to leave behind everything we don't absolutely need."

They rummaged through their pockets and tattered bundles, placing their meager belongings in a heap. There were three Stens—no ammo; a Beretta— no ammo; two Mausers—bayoneted; four stilettos; one switchblade. Thirteen sheets of tobacco paper— no tobacco. A box containing seven matches. A length of piano wire. A frayed rope. That was all.

"Should we take the guns?" Nina asked. "Maybe we can pick up some ammo if—"

"Not the Stens," Janek said firmly. "Ammunition won't be easy to come by. If you find the ammo, you'll find another Sten. The Beretta, yes; it can be used as a club. The Mausers, yes. Knives we'll divide . . . switchblade to Nina. Trina, you take one of the Mausers. Irena, you take the other. I'll keep the Beretta. Irena will take the wire. The rope's too frayed to be of any use. We'll split the matches. . . . That's all, I guess."

It was time to go. Janek turned to Staszek. "Ready?"

"Ready. Trina, take the boots now."

Trina unlaced the heavy shoes, eased them off Staszek's feet, and pulled them over her own. She laced the left boot as tightly as she could to brace her ankle. When she stood up and took a few tentative steps, the pain made her wince, but with the help of Staszek's boot she'd make it.

At last they were ready to move on. As one they faced Staszek. *"Idź z Bogiem . . . z Bogiem . . . z Bogiem*—go with God," they said softly. Then they turned away. All but Janek. The girls waited in silence. And then Janek was with them, saying, "It's done. Let's go."

They moved forward slowly, as if in a dream. The gray tunnel walls seemed to stretch into infinity. Moisture glistened on the walls; the air was acrid, foul, and hard to breathe. Here and there the murkiness was dissipated by lighter patches marking the grilled openings above.

They had been traveling for hours when Janek finally called a halt. "We'll rest here until it's dark," he said, nodding toward the sky visible through the grill overhead. At the next cross street we'll have to climb out. The left turn leads straight into the Vistula, and the right back into the city. We've come as far as we can underground. Remember—when we get up there, we go for the woods. Now, rest."

They sank down onto the concrete and huddled together not so much for warmth, but out of an unspoken need for closeness. They lay dozing fitfully, alert for the slightest sound, listening and waiting. Time passed slowly, marked by the steady *drip . . . drip . . . drip* of falling moisture.

At last Janek stirred. The sky above the grill had turned dark. Janek touched Irena's arm and pointed. There was a faint grating sound as she pushed at the grill. They froze. Slowly, carefully, she pushed again.

Janek was the first one out. "All clear. Come out," he whispered.

One by one they climbed out and ran for the cover of nearby walls. Like moths they fluttered from rubble heap to rubble heap, heading for the woods beyond the city.

Trina was limping badly. Nina grabbed her hand and pulled her along. Finally, when it seemed impossible to go any further, they reached the tall trees. They fell onto the wet grass and drew huge gulps of air. But Janek wouldn't let them stop. They had to keep going. Deeper into the woods, deeper, deeper.

Finally Janek called a halt. The Gray Knights embraced fiercely, in silence. Then Janek and Irena vanished into the woods.

Trina and Nina headed south, watching the stars in order to keep their bearings. By dawn they had crossed the woods. They burrowed into a thick clump of bushes and slept.

The sun was far in the west when they awoke. They were hungry and thirsty. Trina's ankle was throbbing with pain. Nina got up and started to crawl out of the thicket.

"Where are you going?" Trina whispered.

"To look for food."

Before Trina could protest, Nina was gone. She closed her eyes again. Soon Nina was shaking her awake. "Look! Mushrooms!" Nina cried.

The girls munched slowly, savoring every bite. Dew fell, and they ran their hands over the wet leaves and licked them.

When it was completely dark again, the girls started working their way across the fields. They didn't dare use the roads, because the roads were choked with Germans retreating before the Russian advance.

The rough terrain made progress nearly impossible. Trina's ankle slowed her down more and more. She knew that Nina was also in pain and needed a doctor to tend to her hand and her festering neck but when she begged her friend to go on alone, Nina refused.

"Don't waste your breath, Trina," she said firmly. "We're going back together."

Finally, Nina hollowed out a space at the top of a haystack and pushed Trina into it. Then she disappeared into the darkness. Trina slept fitfully, alternately shivering and burning with fever. In the distance dogs were barking. "There must be a village nearby," Trina thought dimly. Barking dogs meant a village.

Nina came back, bringing a man from the village with her. Much later she told Trina that she had sat in a ditch just outside the village for a long time, debating whether to risk going for the help she knew they must have; whether to turn back and try to carry Trina; or whether to just keep going. In the end, she'd decided to knock at the nearest door. The farmer who had answered had been shocked by the gaunt and ragged figure in his doorway. But, after hearing Nina's story, he had quickly harnessed a horse to a wagon, filled the wagon with manure, and headed for the haystack.

Trina lay on the kitchen table. An oil lamp burned nearby, illuminating a circle of solemn faces: the farmer's, his wife's, their children's, Nina's, and that of the village *dziad*—the healer. Trina's left boot was off, and the *dziad* was turning her foot this way and that. It was swollen grotesquely and oozing pus. Trina retched at the fetid smell.

Finally the healer said, "I'll have to clean it. Then I'll see what can be done."

The farmer handed a bottle to Trina. "Drink," he said.

She swallowed, gagged, then drank again. In the meantime, the farmer's wife placed the lamp at the edge of the table. The *dziad* produced a penknife and a bullet. With the point of the knife, he carefully extracted the powder from the bullet. Then he heated the knife in the lamp's flame, sliced across the swelling, and shook the powder into the wound and lit it. As he began to cut and scrape the decaying flesh, Trina fainted.

She woke up surrounded by walls of stacked hay. Sunlight was streaming through chinks in the roof. Nina was asleep beside her, curled in the hay. When Trina touched her, she jumped.

"It's only me," Trina said. "Where are we, and how did we get here?"

"You've been delirious for days," Nina said, and she went on to remind her friend about the farmer and the *dziad*. "The healer worked on my hand and on my burns, too," she added, touching her neck. "Then they hid us here. The woman has been bringing food. The *dziad's* been here to change dressings. They asked us to stay out of sight, because of the Germans."

Two days later, Trina could finally stand up. After dark the girls left the barn and went to the lamplit kitchen. They were ready to leave. The farmer's wife handed them handkerchief-wrapped bundles containing bread, slices of smoked meat, and apples. The farmer said, "There are troops everywhere. If you're going to Radom, you'll have to cross the Pilica. They say that the bridge is gone. Even if it was still there you couldn't use it—there'd be patrols."

"We'll have to decide what to do when we get there," Nina said.

"Z Bogiem . . . z Bogiem."

Fortified by food and rest, Nina and Trina found the going much easier. They reached Mogielnica the first night. Circling the town, they arrived at the banks of the Pilica. To the girls, who couldn't swim a stroke, it looked almost impossibly wide. They sat by the riverside among some rushes and debated what to do. A rowboat? Perhaps, if they could find one. There were boats patrolling the water, but if they muffled the oars perhaps they could slip through. They would explore the banks the next night—there was no time now, dawn was coming. They retreated into the thick underbrush.

Toward evening it began to rain. They shivered in the chilly damp, but were thankful for the change in the weather, knowing that under the cover of rain and darkness it would be easier to cross the river.

They began to explore the shore. Nothing; not a

boat in sight. Finally, as they were about to give up, they almost tripped over a door. A huge old door, incongruous and out of place on the riverbank, but so very welcome! They dragged it to the river's edge and eased it into the water. It floated! They waded after it, climbed aboard, lay down, and began paddling, Nina with her one good hand, Trina with both of hers.

It seemed like an eternity before they reached the opposite bank. As they were stepping ashore, they heard engines. Patrol boats! A searchlight swept the shore. They burrowed into the mud, praying that they'd go unnoticed. From afar they must have looked like two heaps of discarded rags, and the boat passed without even slowing down.

They spent the next day shivering under a clump of bushes in the driving rain. Then they were off again on their seemingly endless journey, picking their way in the darkness, moving through potato fields stripped bare, untended sugar beet patches, rows of cabbages still waiting to be picked and looking like so many fantastically turbaned heads. Then across sand dunes prickly with raspberry bushes, bare of fruit and leaves, but armed with wicked thorns. Heading south.

On the third night after crossing the river, Nina stopped suddenly and clutched Trina's arm. "What do you smell?" she asked.

"Tanneries!" Trina exclaimed, sniffing the pungent

air. "Radom! It's the shoe factories—we're there!"

They had made it. They would be home before the night was out. It had taken them eighteen days to travel ninety kilometers.

28

Zeromska Street. A light rain was falling. The black mushroom caps of umbrellas bobbed along the street. Trina and Nina threaded their way through the passersby. Despite the falling rain and the nearness of their destination, they moved slowly. They lingered for a while on the corner of the square near the Church of St. Agnieszka. Trina fought the tightness in her throat. She glanced over at Nina and saw her friend's eyes shining with tears.

"We're almost home," she said. "We're really here."

Their footsteps echoed in the empty *brama;* the *podwórko* beyond was deserted.

"It looks just the same," Nina said, a note of wonder in her voice. "Nothing has changed at all."

Trina climbed the stairs, feeling her knees shake. When she reached the apartment door she bent down and ran her fingers along the baseboard, searching for the key. There was only empty space. Someone was home. She touched the door handle tenderly, tracing the curly grooves in the brass lever; then she pressed it down.

Ronka was in the kitchen, her back to the door. She was removing a heavy, steaming pot from the stove top. Hinges squeaked as Trina pushed the door open. Ronka turned at the sound.

The pot crashed to the floor. Bits of carrot and chunks of potato swam in a puddle of broth. Ronka's hands had flown to her face. Her mouth moved, but no words came out. Trina hurried to her mother and touched her hand. It felt as cold as ice. "It's me, *mamusia,*" she said.

Hot water filled the big wooden tub to the brim. Ronka had borrowed the bathtub from a neighbor and had lugged it home. Trina luxuriated in the feel of clean warm water and soapsuds lapping at her chin. Tosh was spooning warm stew into her mouth while Ronka scrubbed and soaped. Then Ronka rubbed kerosene into Trina's hair and scrubbed some more, cursing at the lice and nits.

Ronka opened her mouth several times to speak, but each time Tosh glanced at her and ever so slightly shook his head. *Not now,* his eyes said, *not now.*

Trina didn't want to talk anyway. She just wanted to sit in the warm bath and be cared for. She felt almost unbearably sleepy.

Trina snuggled under the covers, into the familiar hollow in the straw mattress. The lights were out. The little stove glowed rosily. Tosh sat quietly on the edge of Trina's bed and held her hand. She slept.

Bright sunlight spilled over the walls. Nearby a clock ticked loudly. "So nice," Trina thought drowsily, "so good to be back here." Her eyes wandered over the familiar room. A pile of clothing on a chair beside her bed caught her attention. Squares of blue serge, a few white things that looked like underwear, a pair of long tan stockings, wooden-soled *saboty*. Trina stretched out her hand and pulled the squares of blue serge off the chair. They unfolded into a skirt and a blouse. A dark blue ribbon fell out from among the folds. Trina ran it idly through her fingers. "For my hair," she thought. "I wonder where Ronka got it?" The blue serge looked oddly familiar. It was Tosh's suit, Trina realized suddenly, the one he had worn to her first communion. Ronka must have sewed all night. She fought the prickling at the back of her eyelids.

Trina threw off the covers and swung her feet over the edge of the bed. "How white my legs look," she thought; they seemed nearly as white as the frayed bandage on her left ankle.

Hurrying now, she put on the new clothes. She felt stiff and ill at ease, as if her body didn't belong to her. When she stared into the mirror, a strange face looked back at her.

Trina put her hand to the mirror and traced the outline of her face on the cool glass. She picked up the blue ribbon and tied it around her braids. Then she looked into the mirror again.

Trina and Nina kept returning to the shed long after they realized that the others were not coming back. They sat on the matted straw, hugging their knees, seldom speaking. Lost in their own thoughts, they watched the snow drift in through the chinks in the walls, shivering in the cold, yet unwilling to go home. Day after day they kept their silent vigil.

During those early winter days, Radom seethed with excitement. The German troops were moving through—column after column of silent soldiers marched westward. The grim-faced figures plodding through the slush were quite unlike those who had gone east singing *"Deutschland, Deutschland, über alles, über alles!"* Between the marching columns rolled convoys of trucks, tanks, and jeeps—an army retreating toward the homeland in silence.

From the sidewalks the people of Radom watched. Jeered. Stared. Whistled the Polish national anthem. The *Szwabs* were leaving! The *Szwabs* were finished!

"What are we going to do after the war?" Trina asked Tosh.

Tosh paused for a moment in the act of lifting a spoon to his mouth. They were sitting at the table eating the thin *żur* Ronka had cooked out of a handful of rye flour and a few potatoes she had miraculously found in the empty marketplace. "After the war?" Tosh replied. "We'll go back to Poznań, of course. Your grandmother, your cousins—you do remember your cousins?"

"Not really." Trina shook her head. "That was so long ago—I was just a child then." She resumed eating and did not see the brief expression of pain that crossed Tosh's face. She was totally absorbed in spooning up the soup. Slowly she became aware that Tosh was speaking again.

"There will be schools again. You'll like that, won't you?"

"Schools?" Trina cocked her head, thoughtfully eyeing the bit of potato in her spoon. "Yes, I'll like that," she said slowly. "School." Her eyes smarted as she remembered Irena and Janek and Staszek bent over their books.

Epilogue

Tosh had been right. They did return to Poznań. In February, 1945, after the Germans had been driven out of Poland, by the Russian army, Trina and Ronka made their way to a city laid waste. Miraculously Aunt Helenka's apartment house had escaped destruction.

Some of their friends had left Radom earlier, but Trina and Ronka had delayed their journey home to bury Tosh. He had been gunned down by the retreating SS while he was trying to move the *Sondergericht* files out of the building.

On the day of their departure, Trina went down to the *piwnica* to collect Tosh's "evidence" and found the brick dislodged and the hiding place stripped of its contents. She stood for a while, stunned, and then went, for one last time, to the shed.

She sat down on the dusty straw. She seemed to hear voices whispering. Tosh's voice: "Remember . . . always remember . . . don't forget. Ever . . . ever . . . ever . . ." Trina whispered back, "I will. I will remember. It doesn't matter about the papers . . . I'll make them remember. I promise."

Then she left the shed and hurried toward the *brama* where Ronka stood waiting.

Glossary

Andrzejki	the name of the Polish underground resistance movement during World War II
baba	old woman; grandmother
babie lato	spiderweb
babusia	old woman; grandmother
berek	a tag game
brama	gate
czarnina	a sweet-sour blood soup
derma	Yiddish: skin from the neck of a goose
dobrze	very well
do widzenia	until we meet again
droszka	wagon
dwór	manor house
dziad	a medicine man, old man
grosz	a unit of Polish money (100 groszy = 1 zloty)

Gwiazdor	the bearded, fur-coated Starman who brings gifts on Christmas Eve; the Polish version of Santa Claus
kelnerz	waiter; *kelnerze;* declension of the former used in direct address
kommisariat	police station
koźlaki	a type of mushroom
kurki	a type of mushroom
kvas	a popular Polish noncarbonated sour soft drink
łapki	waterfowl feet; when cooked, served with giblets impaled upon them
machorka	coarse tobacco used to roll cigarettes
maleńka	little one
maslaki	a type of mushroom
mój Bose	my God
mundurek	a sailor-style outfit worn by Polish schoolgirls
nie	no
Niemcy	Germans
ogórek	cucumber
pączki	filled fried cakes, similar to jelly donuts
pan	mister; master

pani	lady; madam—applies to married women only
panie	declension of *pan* used in direct address, with the meaning then closer to "sir" than "mister"
pierogi	a ravioli-like food made with cheese or potato filling and usually eaten with sour cream
pierzyna	a featherbed
pisanki	Easter eggs
piwnica	basement
podwórko	a courtyard
polewina	a buttermilk soup
powstanie	uprising
prawdziwki	a type of mushroom
saboty	wooden soled shoes, brogans
siostry	sisters
Smigus Dingus	the day after Easter in Poland, celebrated by boys chasing girls and dousing them with water
szwabs	cockroaches, derogatory term for Germans
tata	daddy

214

tzimes	Yiddish: a kind of stew incorporating dried fruit
warsztat	workshop
wycinanki	paper cutouts in the shapes of fantastic flowers and beasts
z Bogiem	go with God
zloty	a unit of Polish money
zoftig	plump, often meaning sexily plump
żubrowka	a pale green vodka flavored with buffalo grass
żur	a sour, rye-based soup